"Do you…like this?" s hesitantly.

"Driving a sleigh?" he asked.

"Yah."

He chuckled. "I do like it. It's…a really different experience. I guess you can get used to anything, but I see the allure of horse-drawn vehicles."

"It's a nice thing that it takes more time to get places," she said. "In your truck, it would probably take five minutes to get to the B and B. But in a sleigh on the back roads, it's twenty minutes at least."

"Is the nice part more time with me?" Thad teased.

Her cheeks pinked. "More time to *think*, Thad. More time to prepare yourself, or to pray before you arrive somewhere."

"Right, of course."

She did have a point about slowing down the hustle and bustle of life. It was calmer, slower, and if he had any anxiety, it would drift away on a sleigh ride like this one.

"That's not to say that more time to talk with a friend isn't nice, too," she added after a beat or two of silence.

He cast her a rueful smile. "I agree."

Patricia Johns is a *Publishers Weekly* bestselling author who writes from Alberta, Canada, where she lives with her husband and son. She writes Amish romances that will leave you yearning for a simpler life. You can find her at patriciajohns.com and on social media, where she loves to connect with her readers. Drop by her website and you might find your next read!

Books by Patricia Johns

Love Inspired

Amish Country Matches

The Amish Matchmaking Dilemma
Their Amish Secret
The Amish Marriage Arrangement
An Amish Mother for His Child
Her Pretend Amish Beau
Amish Sleigh Bells

Redemption's Amish Legacies

The Nanny's Amish Family
A Precious Christmas Gift
Wife on His Doorstep
Snowbound with the Amish Bachelor
Blended Amish Blessings
The Amish Matchmaker's Choice

Harlequin Heartwarming

The Butternut Amish B&B

Her Amish Country Valentine
A Single Dad in Amish Country
A Boy's Amish Christmas

Visit the Author Profile page at LoveInspired.com for more titles.

Amish Sleigh Bells

PATRICIA JOHNS

LOVE INSPIRED
INSPIRATIONAL ROMANCE

LOVE INSPIRED®

INSPIRATIONAL ROMANCE

ISBN-13: 978-1-335-93688-2

Amish Sleigh Bells

Copyright © 2024 by Patricia Johns

Recycling programs for this product may not exist in your area.

Love Inspired
22 Adelaide St. West, 41st Floor
Toronto, Ontario M5H 4E3, Canada
www.LoveInspired.com

Printed in Lithuania

MIX
Paper | Supporting responsible forestry
FSC® C021394

But while he thought on these things, behold, the
angel of the Lord appeared unto him in a dream,
saying, Joseph, thou son of David,
fear not to take unto thee Mary thy wife.
—*Matthew* 1:20

To my husband and son.
You are my whole world. I love you!

Chapter One

The wind howled outside the window, whistling past the house in a shimmer of icy, blowing crystals that glittered in the watery December sunlight. Inside the house, all was toasty warm, though, with the stove pipe pinging merrily, and the logs in the black potbellied stove snapping and popping.

Lydia Speicher pushed a steaming mug of black coffee across the worn, scratched wooden tabletop toward her father, who had his arms crossed irritably over his chest.

"The bishop says that Thad Miller is an Amish man who needs our help," she said. "And I agreed to help him."

Lydia had *gratefully* agreed to help him. She loved her parents dearly, but life was getting so predictable lately, and even with Christmas approaching, she'd found herself a little depressed. It wasn't easy being a single woman in her thirties in their community that was so centered on marriage and family.

"He's Beachy Amish," her father muttered, picking up the mug and taking a noisy sip. "That hardly counts—they're just Amish enough to know better."

The Beachy Amish lived very differently from Redemption, Pennsylvania's Old Order Amish. Beachy Amish drove cars and trucks, they had electricity in their homes, and stopped short at TV and radio. They even had internet, although it was limited. The shocking number of concessions to the world's conveniences never ceased to amaze and disappoint Art Speicher, and he had very strong opinions on the matter.

"We need a veterinarian in the community," Lydia's mother, Willa, reminded her husband. "And Dr. Ted is gone for a while to see his daughter. People still need a vet." Willa took a sip from her own mug of coffee— hers taupe with cream. "And we happily use Englisher veterinarians and doctors and dentists…there's no real difference if he's English or he's Beachy Amish. Not to you and me, at least. This man is a large animal vet in our community, and he needs help finding the farms he's servicing."

"Except the Englishers don't call themselves Amish," her father retorted. "Even Paul doesn't call himself Amish."

Willa's lips pressed together in a thin, disapproving line at the mention of their oldest son, who'd jumped the fence and gone English, and Lydia's gaze darted between her parents. Her *daet* didn't like this arrangement much with Lydia helping the Beachy Amish veterinarian, but when Bishop Glick asked, who was Art Speicher to argue?

Outside, an engine rumbled to a stop, and Lydia peeked out from behind the curtains. The driver's side door of a silver, slightly rusted pickup truck opened and a man stepped out into the snowy cold. He was tall, broad shouldered, and had a felt hat on his head, but the hat was fancier than they normally had in these parts. It looked more like a black felt cowboy hat than a proper Amish hat, and while he wore dark-colored pants and suspenders visible beyond an open black woolen coat, the pants weren't broadfall, and his shirt was a startling blue plaid.

"Oh my..." her mother murmured behind her. "Very fancy, indeed."

Lydia had been asked by the bishop to help Dr. Thad Miller find the local farms he'd be serving for the next couple of weeks. Thad didn't know the area, and having directions like "turn west where the old silo used to be" weren't terribly helpful to someone who hadn't lived in the community all his life, and especially not in December when all the fields looked the same under a mantle of snow.

The man looked around, spotted them in the window, and raised his ungloved hand in a wave. He was an attractive man who looked to be in his thirties like Lydia was. He had blue eyes—she noticed from here—and the boots on his feet looked to be scuffed cowboy boots. He was the most scandalous man in suspenders she'd seen in her life.

But he also looked kind, and she approved of kindness. Truly kind people could be found just about anywhere.

"I'd best go introduce myself," Lydia said, and she slipped past her mother and headed to the side door. She slid into her coat and stepped into her boots. Before she opened the door, she picked up her carpet bag that contained her latest crochet project she was working on—just in case there were some slow times while she waited. She might as well make her time count.

"Good morning!" he called in perfect Pennsylvania Dutch. "I'm Thad Miller. The bishop said there was someone named Lydia who could guide me around these back-country roads. Is she home?"

"I'm Lydia," she said, and she found herself feeling just a little bit bashful with this large, good-looking man. It would be easier if he was a little less...everything!

"Good to meet you." Thad held out a hand to shake hers and Lydia stared at him, stunned.

"We don't do that," she said.

"Do what?" He dropped his hand.

"Amish women don't shake hands with men."

"Sorry." Thad smiled ruefully. "There are a few differences, I know. I'll get used to it."

"It's okay," she said. "But I wouldn't be offering to shake hands with any of the wives you meet out here. They won't like it. And neither will their husbands."

"I'll remember that." He did up his coat halfway, the cold seeming to get to him now that he was outside of his still-running vehicle. He was smooth shaven, which probably meant he was single, but with the Beachy Amish, no one could be too sure.

The side door opened and Art appeared on the step with his own coat on. Her father stroked his full gray beard. "Good morning."

"Good morning!" Thad said, and he headed over and shook Art's hand firmly. "I'm Thad Miller."

"Art Speicher."

"Nice to meet you. I'm Dr. Ted's new assistant. I'm covering his time away, and when he comes back I'll be working with him. So you might see me around. I've heard good things about you folks—how neighborly you are, and how helpful."

Art muttered something and cleared his throat. Lydia couldn't help but smother a smile. It was going to be a whole lot harder for her father to be un-neighborly with that kind of introduction. Besides, Thad was offering something different to do with her days instead of her usual housework and crochet. And he would be around their community...that was news!

"I'd like to see where you'll be taking my daughter today," Art said.

"Of course." Thad pulled out a piece of paper. "I'd expect nothing less. But as you know, the bishop can vouch for me, and so can my home congregation. I come with the good opinion of my church, and a degree in veterinarian medicine."

Art pursed his lips, unimpressed.

"I'm visiting only one farm this morning," Thad went on, passing the page over, "and then I'll drop Lydia back off. It's Jake Knussli's place."

Adel, Jake's wife, was the community matchmaker. What would Adel think of Lydia tagging along with this handsome Beachy Amish man? She wasn't sure!

"That's it?" Art asked. "I thought the bishop said you'd be working hard, not hardly working."

Thad gave a half smile as if expecting it to be a joke, but Art didn't even crack a smile. Normally when her father used that line, he was joking. But Lydia knew her father. He could be difficult when it came to his deeply held opinions, and she silently prayed that he wouldn't embarrass her.

Thad chuckled all the same. "Right... Actually, after

that I head back to the clinic. There's paperwork to do, and possibly some cultures to start processing. There are a few clinic appointments, too. There's always work, that's for sure."

Art grunted, and Lydia shuffled her feet. The cold air worked its way around her legs.

"Well, I'd best get moving," Thad said, "if that's okay with you."

Lydia gave her father a reassuring smile. While Thad Miller might not be ideal in any Amish sense, it wasn't like anyone was suggesting him as a marriage partner for her! This was a simple change of pace for a couple of weeks. She loved her parents and enjoyed her charitable work, but she did find herself getting quite bored these days.

"Drive safe," Art said.

"Thank you. I will," Thad said. "Lydia? You ready?"

Lydia went over to the passenger side of the truck, hauled the door open and hopped up into the seat. She had to push aside a black zippered insulated lunch bag. Her heartbeat sped up in excitement. This would certainly be something different to do, and she was looking forward to it. These days her only chance to get out other than her usual routine was when she went with her parents to service, or when she dropped off her crocheted items for those she thought could use them.

"All right, so we're heading to the Knussli farm, out past the Aberdene dairy," Thad said, passing her the piece of paper.

"Oh, *yah*," she said. "Get out on the main road and head south toward the river. That'll get us going in the right direction."

"Okay, then." Thad put the truck into Reverse, and she watched as he spun the steering wheel on the palm of his broad hand and the truck backed up, then they were heading forward again. Driving would never make sense to her.

"So you'll be working around here?" she asked.

"I will be. Dr. Ted just hired me last week."

"You'll like this area. It's a nice community."

"Yeah, I think so." He shot her a smile. "It's nice to be employed, too. I'm looking forward to gaining more experience before I open my own practice. What about you? What are you aiming at?"

"Me?" She felt heat hit her face. "Well… I help people. That's what I contribute around here. I'm not married, and I don't have *kinner*, so I'm free to help where other people aren't."

"Like helping me?" he asked.

"*Yah*. Like helping you."

"Well, I'm certainly grateful," he said, and his smile warmed her middle.

But his question did probe at a tender spot inside of her. What were her goals? She'd always thought she'd get married and have some children, but that hadn't happened so far. She liked to help others, and she truly felt like she was doing *Gott*'s work when she brought her crocheted blankets to shut-ins or new mothers. But she wanted to do more…help more. She just wasn't sure how.

Lydia gave him the directions as they drove along—a turn here, a change of lane there. She knew these roads like the back of her hand. She'd grown up in this area, and she'd never gone farther than visiting an aunt.

"There—turn left," she said.

The clicking signal light came back on again, and Thad made the turn. "Are you looking forward to Christmas?"

That old swell of bittersweet sadness flooded through her. She used to love Christmastime, and she still did, but Christmas was becoming a bigger and bigger reminder of the family of her own she longed for.

"I suppose so," she said. "Are you?"

"I guess." He shot her a grin. "I have a few nieces and nephews, and I get to spoil them a little bit. I enjoy it."

"So do I," she said.

Christmas, though, seemed to be for children. They were excited about the little gifts, and the time off of school. They loved the extra cookies, the big family meals, and the chance to play with cousins. And while Lydia enjoyed all of the family time, too, she didn't look forward to the prying questions from aunts and uncles about eligible men, as if Lydia simply forgot about her lack of a husband and needed the reminder.

"Do you know how to drive?" Thad asked, tugging her out of her thoughts.

"Me?" She shook her head. "No!"

Thad's eyebrows raised, and she found herself noticing his good looks again when he cast a glance her way. If he was less attractive, that question might offend her. He might live with all those Beachy Amish freedoms, but she did not.

"Do you want to learn?" he asked.

"I'm Old Order," she said. "We don't do that, either."

It was far worse than shaking hands!

"I know. I didn't mean for that to sound disrespectful to your way of life," Thad said. "I'm only asking because we'll be driving through the field to vaccinate some calves, and when we get to them, I need someone to distract the mother cow, and someone else to keep the truck close in case I need to jump in. The farmer usually distracts the mother cow for me, and I was hoping you might keep the truck close."

"I don't think I'm supposed to be doing that..." she said. Was she? She wasn't sure.

"Well, someone has to," he replied. "Sometimes it's someone from the family, or a neighbor... But if there isn't anyone else who can do it, I was hoping you might be willing."

"Is it hard?" she asked.

"Not at all. Just...sit in this seat, press on the gas, and don't run anyone over."

A smile tickled her lips. "That's it?"

"That's it."

It didn't seem so hard, and she knew that Amish people helped out with motor vehicles in situations like this one. It wasn't unheard of. But she'd never done it before.

"It should be okay," she said. "You'll show me how it's done, though?"

"Of course." He cast her an easy grin. "You might even have fun."

Thad turned onto the snow-packed gravel side road, and he pulled closer to the side as another truck rumbled past. Lydia Speicher was exactly what he'd expected when Bishop Glick suggested she would be a good guide through these back roads. She was a prim, proper Amish woman who would never fall captive to his charms—if that was the worry. She was from a good Amish family, and she was devoted to her faith.

"Can I ask you something?" Thad asked as he stepped on the gas again.

"I suppose so."

"Didn't you try driving or anything during your Rumspringa?"

While his Beachy community didn't practice Rumspringa, Thad knew that hers did. It was a time of freedom for the youth—literally translated, "running around time." It was a time for teenagers to experience more freedoms so that when they made a choice for the church, it was informed and there were no regrets.

"No, I didn't," Lydia replied. "I got a job at a grocery store, and I stocked shelves. That was my great freedom—working in town."

"Did you enjoy it?" he asked.

"No. Not especially."

"That's too bad," he murmured.

"I didn't need to try all the Englisher things," she said. "I realized while working that job that what I really wanted was a snug little home, *kinner* to love, and a husband of my own. Unfortunately, that didn't happen."

Thad knew it wasn't fair, but young men often didn't see the importance of depth of character. When he was younger, he didn't know how important that trait would be to him later on, either.

"Yet," Thad said.

"Sorry?"

"It hasn't happened yet," he said. "Life isn't over."

"Well, I'm thirty now. I know how I look. I've been told for years that I'm a bit horsey."

Thad started to smile, then stopped. "You are joking, aren't you?"

"No."

Who would have said that—a brother, a teasing kid? Because it wasn't true. She was a beautiful woman, and he'd noticed that about her right away.

"Who on earth told you that?" Thad demanded. "Horsey? I don't know who said that, but it was a bold-faced lie. Lydia, you're regal."

Lydia's lips formed a silent "oh," and she turned to the front again as if in shock. That was probably crossing a line, but it was true all the same.

"All I'm saying is that you shouldn't just give up on the life you want," he said. "Anything you really want is worth working for, right? That's what my *daet* always told me. That's what made me push all the boundaries and go for my DVM."

"DVM?"

"Doctor of Veterinarian Medicine. It's…a lot of schooling. And in our community, most people don't go beyond high school. There's no need. But I knew what I wanted, and I knew it would take a huge amount of work. No one in my community understood what I was doing. But it was worth the effort, you know?"

"And you think me getting married is…like that?" she asked.

Thad chuckled. "Maybe? I don't know! I'm not married, am I?"

"I don't know. I didn't think that beards meant the same thing to you in your community," she said.

Right. With the Old Order Amish, a married man

wore a beard. A single man was shaven. It was a clearer distinction than even Englisher wedding rings!

"Well… I'm single," he said, and somehow that clarification felt important to him.

"How come?" she asked.

"What?"

"How come you aren't married? You're plenty old enough, and you're moderately good looking."

Moderately good looking? He looked over at her with a grin. She had some spunk, this Lydia Speicher.

"I have a feeling that's as close to a compliment as I'm going to get from you."

"It might be." But she smiled back. "Well? I told you why I'm single. What about you?"

"Because—" He was tempted to joke, to say how he was too handsome for women to take seriously or something, but somehow he couldn't make himself do it. "Because the women in my community didn't understand my ambition," he said. "And the women in my college didn't understand my faith."

There were Christians there, but the Beachy Amish were very conservative. No TV. No radio. No social media. And he believed in those values, but no one he met understood them. He was the too-conservative guy who needed a woman who'd understand those values he held dear. But he'd never met anyone who did. It had been lonely.

"Between two worlds," she murmured.

"*Yah*, exactly." It was the opposite of his time here with the Old Order Amish. He was caught between two worlds here, too, but in a different way. Here, he was the riotously liberal guy. Maybe he should just enjoy the irony.

"Well, we do have a matchmaker here in Redemption," Lydia said. "And she might be able to find a match for me yet. Her name is Adel Knussli."

"As in the farm we're headed to?" he asked.

"The very one."

Their first stop, though, was a couple of miles up the road, and when Lydia pointed out the entrance—without any kind of marker besides a sign that read Birdhouses and Simple Furniture, Inquire at the House—he turned in. He never would have found this place without Lydia's help—that was a guarantee.

Thad drove down the long, narrow drive toward the farmhouse. The farm was set up like most Amish farms—a large two-story house out front, and a stable for the horses to the side, with a corral out back, and a pasture. Beyond was a barn, and beyond that another barn—this being a larger beef farm. And spread out past the barns were fields of grazing cattle. The scent of cattle was on the breeze, slipping into the cab of the truck through the ventilation system—it was an old truck. No matter where he encountered that smell—at a huge beef operation, or a small dairy farm in the heart of Amish country—he always got the same pleasant sensation of coming home. He loved working with cattle and horses, and the privilege to work in veterinarian medicine was never lost on him.

Thad pulled to a stop next to the house, and the side door opened. A bearded young farmer came outside, clapping a felt hat onto his head as he emerged from the house. He had a reddish beard and a ready smile. He gave Thad a nod, then squinted, peering at Lydia next to him.

Lydia waved, and the man nodded. This would be Jake Knussli—the owner of the family-run farm.

"Do you think we'll have time for me to say hello to Adel?" Lydia asked.

"I think so," Thad said. "Can we just see if there's someone to help out with the truck first? If not, I'll need your help."

"It'll work just fine." A smile lit up her features and his heart stuttered in his chest.

Horsey, my foot, he thought to himself. She was gorgeous.

Thad pushed open the truck door, letting in a rush of chilly winter air.

"Good morning!" Thad called.

"Good morning," Jake Knussli called back.

Thad introduced himself, and there was all the small talk about Dr. Ted's new grandbabies and Thad's time there so close to Christmas. Jake said hello to Lydia and asked about her parents.

"Have you got another man around to help keep the truck close while we work with the cattle?" Thad asked.

"I'm sorry, I don't," Jake said. "I just have my wife in the house, but she's with the little ones."

"It's okay," Lydia said. "She's got a three-year-old and a baby in arms. I'll help out."

Thad shot her a grateful smile. He was glad she'd be along for the work—he found he enjoyed her company.

Jake got into the back of the truck and they drove slowly down the gravel drive that led past the barns and toward the fields. Jake hopped down to open and close gates, and then hopped back up again. As Jake held the last gate and Thad drove through, the Amish man pointed out the cluster of cows they'd be approaching.

"The calf is in the back—you can see the mother eyeing us now," Jake said. "She's a feisty one. She hasn't let me near her calf. It'll have to be a team effort, for sure and certain."

"Good—we'll get close, then I'll get my syringe ready."

Jake hopped up into the back again, the truck bouncing with the weight of him on the tailgate, and Thad stepped on the gas ever so carefully, easing them into the snowy field. Four-wheel drive was a must out here.

"Okay," Thad said, glancing over at Lydia as he drove slowly toward the cattle. "So I'm going to give you a really quick lesson in driving a truck when we get over there. The key is to stay calm, and stamp on the brake if you're not sure. Okay?"

"Which one is the brake?" she asked.

"I'll show you. Don't worry. It's easy."

But he could see the discomfort on her face. She was an Old Order woman, and this was not part of her world. No matter how pleasant she seemed, or how much he enjoyed her company, even something as simple as driving a truck twenty feet was a threat to everything she held dear.

Thad was no longer the conservative man out in the world. Now, he was the worldly influence. How was that for irony?

Chapter Two

Thad slowed, steering his truck around a dip in the snow. It was hard to tell how deep those dips went underneath the glittering crust of snow. He glanced over at Lydia. She looked sober—maybe even a little worried. He eased to a stop a few yards away from the cows when the herd started to lumber away from the silage-filled feed ring.

Thad reached into the narrow back seat of the pickup truck and pulled out his insulated medication bag. He opened it, revealing clear glass vials and packaged syringes. He could feel the truck move as Jake hopped out of the back and came ambling past, toward the herd. Jake stopped, his legs akimbo, and surveyed the cattle.

Thad flicked a syringe, replaced the cap over the needle, and put everything back into the bag. Then he shot Lydia a smile.

"Ready to learn to drive?" he asked.

"All right." She was frowning still, though.

"I think it'll be fine," he said. "Come around to this side." He opened the door.

Lydia slid out into the crunching snow and then headed around the back of the rumbling vehicle, and Thad got out and waited for her.

"Hop up into the driver's seat," Thad said. "And put on the seat belt."

Lydia climbed up into the driver's seat, but her legs weren't as long as Thad's, so he reached under the seat to release it, and muscled it forward so she could reach properly.

"Now, this stick here behind the steering wheel is called the shifter. It's how we change the direction the truck goes. Right now, it's in Park—you see the *P* up here on the dash is lit up? That's because we're in Park. So we're not going anywhere. When you put it into Drive, it goes forward. If you need to back up, you'll put it into Reverse…"

It was a quick lesson—about as fast as the first lesson he'd gotten on a tractor on his grandfather's farm when he was about ten.

"When you take your foot off the brake, you'll use the same foot on the gas," Thad said. "This other foot—" He tapped her shin. "This does nothing. Never use it for any pedals. Got it?"

"Okay…"

"Now, put the truck into Drive, but keep your foot on the brake."

Again, she did as she was told, and he took her through it a couple more times—Drive, Reverse, Park. Drive, Reverse, Park. She had it.

Jake came over to watch, his arms crossed over his broad chest.

"Okay, you're ready," Thad said, and he lowered the driver's side window, then slammed the door shut. "Now, I need you to just crawl forward really slowly, and stay as close as you can to the herd. If we need to jump into the truck, you've got to be close. Got it?"

"I'll try," she said.

"And don't drive into the fence," Jake called out merrily. "That's a bother and a half to fix!"

Thad chuckled at the man's humor, and as he headed toward the herd, he glanced over his shoulder. The truck started crawling and then lurched forward. Then it stopped, and Lydia sat there with a white-knuckled grip. She really couldn't do anything too bad out here in a snowy pasture.

"Yeah, that's good!" Thad called. "Try again, a little easier on the gas this time."

The cattle lumbered away from him, moving only as far as they had to. One cow stared at him, chewing her cud, as he headed past her. The mama cow was beyond, and she was staring Thad down with an irritated look in her eye. Her calf—a black-and-white male—was behind her.

Jake picked up a long branch that had fallen from a nearby tree and he stripped some twigs off of it and headed the cow off again, the calf temporarily alone. Thad walked briskly over, straddled the animal, pulled out the syringe, bent over and administered the vaccine, and then released the calf that went bawling back toward its mother.

The cow, however, was not appeased! She lowered her head and beelined straight toward Jake, who jumped out of the way, and then she veered off toward Thad. This mama was bent on revenge!

"Thad!" Lydia shouted out the window.

He didn't need the warning, but he broke into a run,

dashing toward the truck, and he leapt into the back a moment before Jake did.

"Drive, drive!" Thad shouted, and the whole vehicle quivered and squealed. Then the truck lurched forward about twenty feet and suddenly, it tipped, as if a front wheel had dropped into a hole, and the whole vehicle went sideways, the wheels spinning.

Thad jumped down and headed over to the driver's side. Lydia had taken her foot off the gas, and she looked over at him, wide-eyed and white faced.

"It's okay," he said, and he pulled open the door. "These things happen."

She undid the seat belt and nearly pushed him aside, she seemed so eager to get out of the truck.

"I'm sorry!" she said. "I don't know what happened! I'm so sorry!"

Thad looked back. The cattle all looked surprised, standing motionless and watching. At least the mama had stopped her attack and she was in the back of the herd again with her newly vaccinated calf.

"I'm sorry," she repeated.

"Lydia, it's okay," Thad said, and he reached forward, put the truck into neutral, and started rocking the truck back and forth. "Jake, can you push from behind?"

Jake complied, and after a few tries, they eased the truck's wheel out of the hole and Thad steered it to the left and away from it. And while Thad was definitely concerned for his vehicle, his more immediate worry was for the ashen-faced Lydia.

"That's why I drive a pickup—for times like this," Thad said, shooting her a reassuring smile. "This is a pretty tough truck. It's been through a lot with me. It's fine."

And he sincerely hoped it would be, because the last thing he wanted to do was make her feel bad. It wasn't her fault—he was the one who'd asked her to help him.

Thad got into the driver's seat and drove forward a few yards. He could hear a funny clunking sound—that wasn't a good sign. He stopped a good distance from the cows and got back out. He laid down on his back in the snow and slid under the front fender to see if he could spot the problem. But he wasn't a mechanic—even though he should probably learn more about fixing his own truck if he was going to be working out here in the sticks.

Thad shimmied back out from under the truck, and when he emerged, he was met with Lydia's solemn stare. She stood to one side, her boots pressed close together, and her arms crossed as she surveyed him carefully, watching his expression.

"I broke it, didn't I?" Lydia asked.

"No! Of course not." He felt uncomfortable under her direct stare.

"Don't lie to spare my feelings, Thad," she said. "If I've broken your truck, then I should pay for the damage. The Good Book says that the truth sets us free."

As if he'd charge Lydia for the damage to his vehicle. The Good Book also said to do unto others as he'd have them do unto him. And charging someone for an accident didn't sound like a kind thing to do.

"I have insurance, Lydia," he said gently. "You really don't need to worry about this. I promise."

Her eyes widened. Yes, another difference. The Old

Order Amish didn't believe in insurance—they believed in community, and if they needed help paying for an accident or a misfortune, then the community came together and pooled their resources. It was an insurance of sorts, he supposed. But for everyone else, it was illegal to drive a motor vehicle without proper, certified motor vehicle insurance.

"So I did break it?" Lydia asked, and her face paled.

"Things happen, Lydia. It could have been me behind the wheel, and we'd still have hit that hole. It wasn't visible from the driver's seat and covered by snow."

"So I did…" She sighed and dropped her arms to her side. "I feel terrible. I do."

"Well, don't!" He pushed himself to his feet and brushed off the back of his pants. There were a few more calves to vaccinate still, but he had a feeling that he and Jake would do better alone. Lydia looked too upset. "Look, your friend is in the house, right?"

Lydia's gaze moved in that direction. *"Yah."*

"Why don't you go inside and warm up, have a cup of coffee or something, and I'll come get you when we're done out here."

She nodded. "Okay."

"Do you need a ride back?" Thad asked.

Lydia gave a rueful smile. "I can walk."

Right. She wasn't exactly helpless. She turned without another word and headed back toward the farmhouse, her dress rippling around her legs in the winter wind. Her shoulders were hunched up, and she looked cold. He wished she'd accepted the ride.

"All right," Thad said, tearing his attention away from

Lydia and turning back to the task at hand. "Where is the next calf?"

There was work to be done, but he couldn't help but wonder if he'd ruined things with Lydia as his navigator so soon. He'd been wrong to ask her to drive. This wasn't about rules and whether or not her bishop would allow her to help out. This was about Lydia's personal comfort level—and Thad had a sinking feeling that he'd messed that up already.

Lydia walked a little faster as she headed across the field toward the gate. Let the men vaccinate calves—she'd done enough damage already, and her heart was hammering in her throat.

"That's why we don't drive motor vehicles!" she muttered to herself. "They're too fast! They're too dangerous!"

Although she knew that wasn't really the reason. Horses could be both fast and dangerous, too. It had to do with how far a person could travel, and a horse and buggy made it so that a person could comfortably go about ten miles from home. More than that got strenuous on both man and beast. Horse power—the literal kind—kept a community closer together and more reliant on each other. It was about preserving their lifestyle. And if that accident with the truck had shown her anything today, it was that they were right about slowing down. And she should never have been behind that wheel.

But Thad was handsome and friendly, and he said nice things to her. She'd just wanted to please him, and she was kicking herself for that now. Was she really this susceptible to flattery?

Lydia stomped through the snow toward the house

and the welcoming scent of wood smoke from the chimney. She spotted Adel in the window, the baby on her hip, then her friend disappeared, and a moment later the side door opened.

"Hello!" Adel called. "Are you all right, Lydia?"

Adel backed inside and the screen door shut, but Lydia knew it was for the warmth. Lydia came up the steps, kicking snow off her boots, and she pulled open the screen and stepped into Adel's mudroom. Samuel, Adel's three-year-old son, leaned against the wall and watched her with big eyes. Adel popped her baby boy, Levi, up on her hip. He was about four months old now, and looked a lot like his big brother with the same big eyes and pink lips.

"I broke his truck," Lydia announced, shutting the door solidly behind her.

"What?" Adel blinked at her. "What are you talking about?"

"They needed me to drive the truck a few yards while they distracted the cow and gave the vaccine. And in that amount of time, I've broken it!" Lydia shivered as she peeled off her coat. "I'm the one who helps people, Adel. That's what I do. When people need something in our community, the bishop always knows I can be counted on. And what do I do? I break the man's truck!"

"Well, get your boots off and come by the stove," Adel said. She looked over her shoulder and winced. "It's a mess, I'm afraid."

"I won't judge," Lydia said with a smile, and she stepped out of her boots and came into the warm kitchen. But Adel hadn't been exaggerating. The room was a mess—no other way to say it! There was a hamper of dirty laundry waiting by the basement door. It looked to be laundry for the baby—little sleepers and onesies, cloths and baby blankets. The oatmeal bowls from breakfast were still on the table, as was a pile of flyers from their mailbox, Lydia assumed. That was the same collection of flyers she'd gotten from their own mailbox that morning. There was a pile of dishes in the sink, a plate with a half-eaten muffin on the floor next to some toys that Samuel must have been playing with, and the floor looked like it needed a mop because of the little puddles that must have been from snow on boots.

Tears welled in Adel's eyes as Lydia's gaze moved around the room.

"Adel, are you all right?" Lydia asked, crossing the room and stopping in front of her friend.

"I'm a bit overwhelmed," Adel said. "I know it's messy. I'd have cleaned if I knew you were coming."

"I'm sorry to just barge in," Lydia said.

But tears about a messy kitchen from Adel were certainly not the norm. Adel was the strongest woman Lydia knew. She seemed to support all of the women of Redemption with her advice and matter-of-fact wisdom. But it looked to Lydia like Adel was struggling.

"You sit down," Lydia said. "I'll clean up a bit."

"No!" Adel's eyes flashed. "I can take care of it. I just got a late start, is all. Here, would you hold Levi? He's been fussy, and he's up four times a night again like when he was a newborn."

Lydia accepted the baby and snuggled him close. She moved closer to the stove for warmth, and Adel started taking the dishes off the table, bowls thunking as she piled them up.

"He hasn't been sleeping?" Lydia asked.

"Levi is just so clingy," Adel sighed. "It must be the start of teething, but this is so much earlier than Samuel. He was six months before he got like this."

Levi stuffed a hand into his mouth and dribbled drool down his chin and onto his sleeve.

"I know it's hard without your mother to come help out," Lydia said. "And your husband's mother is gone, too. You need a stand-in *mammi*, that's what you need!"

"Oh, I'm fine," Adel said. "I'll get the balance of it."

"Have you been able to get out and see anyone?" Lydia asked.

"I don't have the time!" Adel said. "I'm getting ready for Christmas and my sister's visit, and Samuel has started being very naughty. I'm not sure if he's feeling jealous of the baby, or what, but it's been hard."

That had been said in English, so Samuel wouldn't understand it. Like most Amish children, he knew one language until he went to school, and that was Pennsylvania Dutch. Samuel went over to where his mother stood by the sink and reached up and tugged on her apron. She looked down at him and then gathered him up in her arms.

"Oh, my sweet boy," Adel sighed, reverting back to their native tongue.

Samuel leaned his head against his mother's shoulder, his lower lip quivering.

"Naomi is coming for Christmas?" Lydia asked with a smile, trying to lighten the mood, if only for little Samuel.

"*Yah*, she and Mose are coming with their little girl."

"How old is the baby now?" Lydia asked.

"Hannah Marie is eight months." Adel smiled wistfully. "I'm glad they finally got the baby they were praying for. And it will be so nice to see my sister again. In fact, we want to have all of you come by on Second Christmas to visit with us. Naomi has missed you so much."

"I'd be happy to come," she said. "I've missed Naomi, too."

"She says she'll make some of her cinnamon rolls," Adel added. "I've missed those, too. No one makes cinnamon rolls like Naomi."

"Have you been doing any matchmaking?" Lydia asked, afraid of sounding too pushy, but she did want to know.

"Oh, Lydia…" Adel put a hand over her eyes. "I'm sorry. I haven't been. I'm just so busy, busy, busy all the time." She dropped her hand. "But you are my very next priority in my matchmaking. I promise you."

Lydia was the last of the six women Adel had tried to set Jake up with before Adel married him herself, and she'd taken her responsibility to find each of them loving husbands very seriously. The other five were married now, and Lydia had been hoping that Adel might have some man tucked away somewhere who'd be perfect for her. But so far, there had been no hint.

"Am I very hard to match?" Lydia asked.

Adel shook her head. "You're wonderful, Lydia! I just have to find the right man who will treat you with love and respect."

A man who would see past her plain face. That was the problem. But Thad had said she was regal… Did that mean pretty? It certainly wasn't a bad thing… She'd never been told that she looked regal before! Did he really think so, or was that some sort of Beachy Amish politeness? But it would seem that Adel didn't have some nice, available man tucked away somewhere, and it felt selfish of her to even be asking about it.

"Well, don't you worry about me," Lydia said. "You've got your hands full with your own family."

And how Lydia wished she could be busy with her own husband and *kinner*. She knew it was a lot of work, but what a blessing to have that work, too!

"Lydia, I haven't forgotten about you," Adel said, and she put Samuel back down on the ground, and turned back to the kitchen sink. The pots clattered as she moved them aside and put in the plug. "I'm going to write some letters to some communities in Indiana and Ohio asking about eligible men looking for wives. There's that community in Oregon, too, where Adam Lantz came from, and my sister mentioned that she'd heard there were some Amish men working in some factories in their area in Ohio who are still single. But they might be too young…" Adel winced. "I haven't forgotten you, Lydia. I promise."

It seemed that Adel was going to have to really roll up her sleeves if she wanted to find someone for Lydia, though, and the thought was a little disheartening.

Lydia put Levi into his high chair at the table and did up the strap to hold him in. She arranged a blanket around him, then handed him a spoon that he immediately dropped on the ground. Lydia picked it up, and Levi's little mouth twisted into a wail.

"You take Levi," Lydia said. "I'll do dishes."

"I just—" Adel stepped away from the sink and headed over to her wailing baby. She scooped him up and started to gently bounce him. "I just need some time to myself where no one touches me. Is that terrible? Lydia, be truthful. Am I awful?"

"My little sister complains about the same things," Lydia replied. "There is nothing wrong with you, Adel. You're tired! And this is a hard season. That's all."

"Oh, I hope so." Adel sank into a kitchen chair, and Samuel tried to get up into his mother's lap, too. Adel hoisted him up, and leaned back in the chair. Her face was pale and she cast Lydia a faint smile.

"Let me fill you in on the news," Lydia said brightly, and she headed over to the sink and turned off the water. "Bishop Glick asked if I'd help the Beachy Amish veterinarian navigate—you knew that, right? Well, my *daet* is not well pleased about me driving around with him. *Daet* has all sorts of issues with the Beachy Amish way of living. He says they're lukewarm, but my *mamm* likes to see me get out and do something different..."

As Lydia washed dishes, rinsed them, and put them in the dish rack, she chattered away to Adel about her parents and this new Beachy Amish veterinarian, who was truly the biggest bit of news Lydia had these days. She hadn't been getting out too often, either.

"What's he like?" Adel asked.

"He's nice," Lydia said, rinsing a pot. It was too big to go onto the dish rack, so she grabbed a tea towel and started to wipe it dry. "He's...complimentary."

"To you?" Adel asked.

"*Yah*, to me. He says nice things, and he appears to mean them. I brought my crocheting with me in case I needed to fill time, but he seems very chatty. I don't think I'll need it."

Adel smiled. "He seems to like you."

"He's just friendly."

"Single men are not that friendly with single women if they don't like them," Adel said.

"He's Beachy..."

"There is that." Adel nodded. "But it must be nice to have someone new to talk to, all the same."

"It is," Lydia agreed, putting the dry pot on the counter and turning back to the sink. "I've been getting rather bored, you know. Everything has been the same day in and day out. I cook and clean with *Mamm*, and I crochet my little stuffed animals for the local *kinner*, and I make afghans for the older folks. I go to church on Service Sundays. I do love my life, but..."

"You're ready for more," Adel said quietly.

"I am ready for more." Lydia plunged her hands back into the sudsy water. "But more will come when *Gott* wills it. What can I do?"

The rumble of Thad's truck could be heard outside, and Lydia and Adel both looked toward the window. The snow had stopped falling, and the sound of the engine grew steadily louder.

"It's time for you to go, I think," Adel said, and she planted a kiss on Samuel's cheek and put him down as she rose to her feet. "Don't worry, Lydia. I'll be okay. Jake will help me get things cleaned up, and it's almost time for Levi's nap. After I feed him, he should sleep for a couple of hours. I'll get it all done."

Lydia dried her hands and cast her friend a sympathetic smile. "Do you want me to come back and help out?"

"You're busy helping that Beachy Amish veterinarian," Adel replied. "Don't worry. You just caught me at an emotional moment. I feel silly now for saying anything at all. I'm fine, I promise. You'd better hurry, though."

Adel was far from "fine," and Lydia knew it, but she was also right. Lydia had already promised her time to helping out the temporary vet. But she worried about her friend all the same.

"You're a good *mamm*," Lydia said, giving Adel a gentle side hug. Then she bent down and ruffled Samuel's hair. "You're doing a good job, Adel."

Adel smiled faintly, and Lydia headed for her coat and boots once more. It wasn't easy being single, but it wasn't easy being a married mother, either. It seemed like a woman had to choose her difficult path, but for some women, like Lydia, there hadn't ever been a choice. She knew that marriage and motherhood had their own challenges, but so did the loneliness of the single life. So Lydia prayed for her own challenges—a husband and some *kinner*. If only she could be so blessed.

Chapter Three

❦

Thad pulled to a stop next to the house. The truck was making a thunking noise now when he drove, and that was worrisome. Something had broken when the wheel went into that hole in the field, but there wasn't much he could do now besides bring it into the shop. But before he did that, he needed to bring Lydia home, and the truck still seemed drivable. This would probably be an expensive fix, though.

"*Danke* for everything," Jake said. "I appreciate it."

"My pleasure," Thad replied. "Nice to meet you, too."

The house's side door opened, and Lydia came outside, her breath fogging in the air. She turned and waved, then pulled the door shut behind her and came down the steps toward the truck.

Jake hopped out of the truck as Lydia approached.

"Jake," Lydia said, and she lowered her voice, but Thad could still hear her words. "Adel seems like she's having a tough time right now."

"She's tired, I know," Jake said.

"No, she's more than tired. She's completely overwhelmed. I think she might be depressed."

Jake stood motionless, and he looked back at Thad, his eyes swimming with worry.

"I'll take care of her," Jake said. "She's not sleeping enough. That's the problem. I'll take over with the *kinner* this afternoon and let her get some rest."

"That might help," Lydia said, but she didn't sound convinced. "She could use the rest."

Lydia got up into the truck, and Jake headed into his house. As Thad stepped on the gas and headed toward the drive, he glanced over at Lydia. Her expression was sober.

"How is your friend?" he asked as he pulled onto the road. That clunking sound was still there, and he couldn't help but focus on it. Should he have left the truck here and called for roadside assistance or something? No doubt, this farmer would have gotten Lydia back home again.

"I'm still worried about her," Lydia said. "Adel is the strongest woman I know, but she's been working too hard lately. She's got two little ones—a little boy and a baby. That's not too much to deal with, but she's also our local matchmaker, and she takes that role very seriously, too. When she should be resting, she's taking on other worries."

"That's right, you mentioned she was a matchmaker," he said.

That was a strange thought—something they didn't have in his community. But the Old Order Amish were a very practical people.

"She's well-respected, too," Lydia said. "She's found matches for all sorts of women in our area, and they're deeply grateful. She's been feeling rather low, though.

So I think I'll get some ladies together to go visit her soon—a little sunshine party."

"Is that a thing?" he asked.

"A sunshine party?" she asked. "Of course! It's when someone needs cheering, and we all go over to visit. We bring desserts and little gifts, and if she needs help getting caught up on her housework, we all pitch in until her home positively gleams. It's easier to feel pulled together when your home is pulled together."

That clunking got worse the faster he drove, so Thad slowed down to under the speed limit. Sometimes he envied the Old Order Amish for their simple way of life, where a matchmaker could find a good marriage match for someone who was otherwise struggling. The Beachy Amish just did their best like anyone else.

"Turn left here," Lydia said. She didn't seem to notice the odd sound, but then maybe someone needed to know vehicles better to hear when something was off.

Thad signaled and made the turn. He recognized the road where the Speichers lived. He and Lydia were almost back. But when he finally pulled up next to the house, he felt something in the truck slip, and there was a final clunk that left him with a foreboding feeling.

"I think I'd better call that tow truck," Thad said more to himself than to Lydia.

But at least he'd gotten Lydia home.

An hour later, Thad leaned against his truck, his phone against his ear. A tow truck was on its way...well, within a three-hour window, so it would come eventually. At least he wasn't stuck on the side of the road somewhere, and he was relatively certain that the Speichers would feed him.

"Hello, sir, I double-checked," the woman from the car rental agency said over the phone, "but we don't have anything larger than a mid-sized sedan available."

"A sedan."

"Yes, sir. Would you like me to reserve one?"

"No, that won't do. I'm a large animal veterinarian. I'm driving from farm to farm. I'm out in fields. A sedan won't be tough enough."

"I'm really sorry, sir. But there is a big stampede going on right now, and all of our trucks have been rented."

"Well, thanks all the same," he said.

That was the fourth car rental place he'd called, and they all were saying the same thing—they had no pickup trucks available for rent. There were some cube vans—which would not do—and smaller cars. But neither of those were an option for his job.

The timing for this damage to his truck couldn't be worse, but he didn't want to let Lydia know that. She already felt bad enough as it was. And it wasn't her fault—it could have happened to anyone, and he'd been the one who'd asked her to be behind the wheel. This was entirely on him.

The side door opened, and Lydia came outside with a shawl around her shoulders, boots on her feet, and a white plate held in front of her. Was that a donut? No, it was two donuts! He couldn't help but smile. She crossed the snow and held the plate out to him and he pocketed the phone.

"Thanks," he said. "This looks great."

"*Mamm* made a big batch of donuts today," Lydia said. "She's famous for them in these parts."

Thad took a bite of a honey-glazed donut, and it melted in his mouth. It was delicious. He hadn't tasted better...ever!

"She should sell these," he said, taking another bite.

"No, not *Mamm*. She says there has to be a perk for being loved by her, and her donuts are one of those perks."

Thad shot her a smile while chewing another bite. "I like that."

"So do we. We have the best donuts around any time she's in the mood to make them."

"Did she teach you how?" he asked, catching her eye.

Lydia's cheeks grew pink. "*Yah*, she did. And there is a perk for the man I eventually marry, too."

Thad chuckled at her humor. He licked off his fingers and handed the plate back.

"Whatever man you marry will be blessed to have you, Lydia," he said.

"Is everything all right out here?" Lydia asked. "We've been watching you pacing around with that phone of yours for the last half hour. *Mamm* wanted me to bring you inside for some lunch."

Lunch was certainly tempting, and Thad glanced in the direction of the house.

"It might be a few hours before the tow truck comes out here," Thad replied. "I wouldn't turn down a meal, that's for sure. But you might be stuck with me for a little bit."

"That's no bother." Lydia paused. "You should come inside. *Mamm* has some soup on, and there's ham sandwiches, too."

Thad's stomach rumbled in reply. He'd planned to stop in town at a restaurant for some quick lunch, but it didn't look like that would be possible now.

"Don't mind if I do," Thad said. "I appreciate it."

Lydia led the way back toward the house.

"I'm trying to rent another truck until mine is fixed," he said as they headed up the steps and inside through the side door. "It'll be a few days at least. And I'm not able to find any trucks available. There's a big stampede going on right now, and the pickups are all rented."

"Oh, that's too bad," Lydia said. "I don't mind saying, that's another good reason we don't rely on gas vehicles. A buggy runs just fine as long as there's a horse to pull it. And if you don't have a horse, you neighbor will lend you one."

A buggy… They were quick, rolled over pretty much any terrain as long as the horse could get through… He could bring a buggy out into a field, if he needed to. But he had no idea how to drive one, let alone hitch it up. Thad took off his hat and hung it on a peg by the door, and pushed the door shut behind them.

"Oh, Lydia, don't preach at him now about a proper, plain lifestyle," her mother said, shooting him a disarming smile. "Our decent ways should speak for themselves. No need to hound him. I'm Willa, by the way. You've met my husband, Art."

Thad couldn't help but chuckle. Yes, he was very likely going to be hinted at the whole time he was here about the Old Order way of doing things, wasn't he?

"I'm not hounding him," Lydia said. "I was pointing out that our ways are sensible. In fact, I don't see why he couldn't use a buggy while he's working in our area. The rest of us do."

"A buggy, huh?" Thad said thoughtfully.

"Well, where is he staying?" Willa asked.

Both women turned and looked at him, matching expectant looks on their faces.

"At a hotel in Redemption," he said.

"See? That won't do." Willa headed over to the stove and took a lid off a steaming pot. The whole room smelled of tomato soup, and Thad's stomach rumbled again. "You can't have a buggy where there's no stable."

"All he has to do is stay at the Draschel B&B," Lydia said. "They've got a stable there, and they're...five minutes up the road? It's not far."

"That would work," Willa agreed.

"The Draschel B&B?" Thad asked.

"It's a local establishment—Amish run," Lydia explained. "It's actually owned by Adel Knussli—we just came from their farm. But the Knusslis don't run it. They've got the farm to take care of. It was Adel's from her first marriage before her first husband died. She's remarried now to Jake Knussli. But the B&B is now run by the Beiler family."

This was a lot of information that didn't really touch on why he was interested. If he couldn't get a pickup truck, was it crazy to think about using a buggy for a week? Would a buggy's slender wheels really be the best option out in a snow field?

"And I happen to know that they don't have any guests at all right now," Willa added. "I ran into Claire in town yesterday, and she was saying that they're empty for a whole week, which almost never happens."

The side door opened, and Thad turned to see Art Speicher come into the house. His boots thumped on the wooden floor, and he took off his hat and hung it on a peg next to Thad's. Art's hat was simpler, and a little more beaten up than Thad's was.

"That soup smells delicious, Willa," Art called out cheerfully, and came into the kitchen, rubbing a hand over his protruding belly. He pulled out the chair at the head of the table and sat down. "Are you staying for lunch, young doctor?"

"I was hoping to," Thad said. "I'm afraid my truck is giving me trouble. I've called a tow, but it will likely be a little while before it arrives."

"There's a problem with him renting a new one, too," Lydia added, and between Lydia and her mother, they filled her father in on all the pertinent details.

"You broke his truck, Lydia?" Art asked in exasperation.

"I didn't mean to," she said.

"It wasn't her fault," Thad broke in. "I keep telling her that."

"That's what you get for getting behind a wheel, young lady," Art said. "I could lecture you, but I think you learned already."

"Of course, *Daet*," Lydia gave her father a long-suffering look. "I'm not Paul, and I have no longing for those things."

"I can be thankful for that," Art muttered. Then he sighed. "All the same, it seems to me that we are responsible for Thad's current situation."

"No, no, really—" Thad started.

"He should use a buggy," Willa said, cutting Thad

off mid-sentence. "I think it makes sense, but I wanted to ask you, Art. You would know better."

"Well, now…" Art pressed his lips together. "You're a wise woman, Willa. But…are you taking the vehicle out into the fields, Thad?"

"Yes, that's the plan. I suppose I could just walk out there if I'm pressed—"

"A sleigh would be better," Art said.

"A sleigh?" Thad asked in surprise. "What about the roads?"

"Oh, none of the back roads are plowed," Art replied. "You'd have to avoid the main roads, but my daughter could help you there." He turned to his wife and daughter. "I do believe a sleigh would suit his needs nicely so long as the snow keeps falling, and the weather is calling for more of it. Who needs to rumble around in some big truck like that? No one, that's who."

"But he'd need to borrow that sleigh," Lydia put in. "And a horse to pull it."

"Seeing as we're the ones who caused him trouble," Art said, "I suppose we could show this Beachy Amish man the proper Amish way of things."

Thad rubbed a hand over the back of his neck. It seemed to him that the Speicher family was going to sort out a solution for him, whether he wanted their input or not.

"He could stay at the Draschel B&B," Lydia added.

Willa brought a big soup tureen to the table, and then brought another large platter of sandwiches. Thad's stomach rumbled again, and Willa gestured for him to sit down. He pulled out a seat next to Art, and Lydia took the chair opposite his.

"This looks wonderful," Thad said.

"*Danke*, I do enjoy cooking," Willa said with a smile.

Everyone bowed their heads then, and there was a moment of silent grace. Art cleared his throat, and everyone raised their heads, and dishing up commenced.

"Then it's settled," Art said, accepting a bowl of soup from his wife's hands. "We will lend young Thad our sleigh and a horse, and we'll help him move his things over to the B&B."

"I actually don't know how to hitch up or drive a sleigh," Thad said, managing to interject a word for the first time.

Willa handed him a bowl filled with rich tomato soup, with flakes of parsley floating on top.

"I'm rather busy this afternoon," Art said, "but I'm sure Lydia could teach you. It's not hard, you know. Plus, it would seem she owes you."

Thad shot Lydia a wary look, and she shrugged innocently. "I'd be happy to. If that's what you want."

"And maybe you'll see the wisdom of our Old Order ways after all," Art said with a sly little smile. "No one needs to travel that fast or that loudly. No one."

Lydia was hungry after a morning of breaking a man's pickup truck and evading an angry mama cow. But she was rather pleased at the thought of showing Thad how the Old Order Amish did things. And this time of year did make for some pleasant sleigh rides. They'd pulled the sleigh out of the garage last weekend for some sleigh ride fun when some of her nieces and nephews came to visit, so it was all dusted off, waxed up, and ready to use again.

Thad and her father tucked into the food, conversation swallowed up in a hearty meal, and Lydia turned to her mother.

"*Mamm*, we stopped at the Knussli farm today," Lydia said.

"How is Adel doing?" Willa asked. "She's been distant lately."

"I was worried about her, too," Lydia said. "And she's so tired out with the baby and her little boy. The baby is teething and Samuel is getting clingy, and I think she's just overwhelmed. I wouldn't believe it if I didn't see it myself, but our strong, confident Adel is…frazzled."

"One thing I've learned over the years," her mother said softly, "is that we need to check up on our strongest friends. The ones who support everyone else need support, too."

"And Adel needs us," Lydia said seriously.

"I'll talk to some ladies," her mother said with a nod. "You take care of our temporary veterinarian, and I'll gather the ladies to help Adel. We'll go over tonight. If she's struggling now, going over in a few days isn't going to be helpful, is it?"

"I thought a sunshine party might help," Lydia said.

"I agree. We'll bring her some cheer this evening. Sometimes those baby blues descend upon a woman, and she doesn't even realize it. Adel's parents are both gone now, so she doesn't have a *mamm* to notice these things. That's what we women are here for." Willa was silent for a moment. "Did she mention any potential matches for you?"

Lydia shook her head. "No. She's just so busy."

And Lydia's clock was ticking. She'd been hopeful

that their matchmaker would do for her what she'd done for so many other women in their community.

That was an exciting thought, because she'd hoped that meant that her time was close, and she'd finally get her own chance at marriage and motherhood. Unless poor Adel had reached the end of her strength and was about to back away from matchmaking and focus on her own little family.

Who would blame Adel for that, either?

But the thought was achingly disappointing for Lydia, because Adel did feel like her last chance at finding a good Amish husband to spend her days with. Somehow, the years kept slipping by, and there were no suitors knocking. Still, Lydia did have a heart full of love saved up for the man who would be hers…and a very special donut recipe, too.

"Well, when you get Thad over to the B&B, make sure you tell Claire about the sunshine party," Willa said. "We'll meet at the Knussli farm at seven. That would give Adel enough time to finish eating. I'll go round up the other women myself, but if you can tell Claire, it will save me time."

When the meal was over, Lydia helped her mother to clear the table, and then Willa waved her off.

"Go show Thad how to hitch up," Willa said. "I'll take care of the rest."

Lydia led the way outside. Her father had indicated which horse he'd lend to Thad—a nice strong draft horse who knew his way around a bit. Thad followed her outside, and as the screen door bounced shut behind them, Lydia looked over at the stranded veterinarian.

Had they rolled right over him? Her *daet* could be

rather forceful when he decided upon something, and Lydia and Willa had been so focused on solving the problem that Lydia hadn't stopped to ask Thad what he thought about their solution.

"I hope we haven't offended you," Lydia said.

"Hmm?" Thad looked like she'd startled him out of his thoughts.

"I said, I hope we haven't offended you," Lydia repeated. "We do believe very strongly in our way of life, but I know it isn't right for us to push our ways onto you. You were raised differently, and there is no shame in you staying true to the life that your parents raised you to."

"Thanks." He shot her a rueful smile. "I'm not sure your *daet* agrees with you there."

"No, he probably doesn't," she replied. "He thinks that if anyone sat down and thought it through logically enough, they'd end up becoming Old Order Amish."

"Anyone?" he asked.

"Absolutely anyone." She chuckled. "But that's my *daet* for you." She led the way to the stable and opened the door. "So what are your parents like?"

"Well, they're Beachy Amish," he said. "My dad is a mechanic, and my mom is a homemaker. I've got five siblings, three of which stayed in the church."

"Two went English?" she asked in surprise.

"Two went more than English, as you put it," he said quietly. "They lost faith in God altogether."

"Oh…" She exhaled a soft sigh. "Why?"

"I don't know," he said, and after a beat he shook his head. "I think they stopped wanting to believe. That factors into it a lot, you know."

Lydia's mind went back to her brother—Paul, the fun

one, who used to throw snowballs in the winter, and spray her with the pump water in summer. When he'd jumped the fence and left their community, the whole family had grieved for him. But thankfully he did it before he'd made a choice for the church, because that meant he could still come home and visit and they could see him.

"I'm sorry they made that choice," Lydia said. "My brother went English, but he still believes in *Gott*. He and his family attend a church in the city."

"Every family has their struggles," he said.

"*Yah*, that's the truth." Lydia led the way into the stable to fetch the big draft horse, Absalom, and the tack. For a moment Thad hesitated by the door. He was a tall man, and the sunlight glowed behind him.

"We aren't all that different, are we?" Thad asked, then he strode forward and took the heavy tack from her hands and tossed it over one of his big shoulders.

"We are quite different," Lydia countered, "but if you can live a week as Old Order and learn how to hitch your own sleigh, you'll earn my respect."

Thad grinned. "You don't think I can do it, do you?" he asked.

"I'm not sure," she replied. "Our way of life is harder than yours. It takes patience, muscle, hard work."

"I've got patience, some muscle, and a work ethic." A smile toyed at one side of his mouth. She felt her face heat. She hadn't meant to comment on his muscles— that was wildly inappropriate!

"We'll see," she said.

Lydia was teasing him now, but she was partly serious, too. Every once in a while an Englisher tried to live

Amish. They didn't last. The Beachy Amish had conveniences that the Old Order Amish refused to take advantage of. She lifted the last of the heavy leather straps and belts off the wall and put them over her shoulder.

"Now, come on," she said, slipping past him out into the sunlight again. "Let's go get the horse and I'll show you how this works."

"Hold on," Thad said.

She turned back. *"Yah?"*

"I'll carry that for you," he said. "It looks heavy."

It was heavy, and she felt a little self-conscious as she handed it over. He tossed the tack over his other strong shoulder and didn't seem to even notice the weight of it. It was nice to be treated like a woman, and she found herself feeling a little bashful.

Lydia could see her father heading across the field, a tool bag over one shoulder. If Thad could work like an Old Order Amish man for a week, he'd earn her father's respect, too. And maybe even soften her father's feelings toward the Beachy Amish.

They deposited the heavy tack beside the sleigh. The horse followed them into the pasture, and when she handed Thad the bridle, his warm fingers brushed against hers.

"Which horse?" he asked.

"That one—the black draft gelding," she said pointing.

"What's his name?"

"His name is Absalom, because he's so beautiful," she said.

Thad grinned. "All right. And is this a trick? Does he have an attitude or something I should know about?"

"There are no tricks," Lydia replied.

There was no need for trickery. She didn't want Thad to fail, and she didn't want to toy with him, either. She'd already caused damage to his truck, and she truly did want to help him until his vehicle was fixed again. Her father, on the other hand, wanted to prove to Thad that the Old Order way was better.

And her father would have his work cut out for him there, because Thad didn't strike her as a man who was easily swayed in his beliefs.

Thad approached the horse with confidence, and Absalom seemed to take to him right away. Thad probably worked with horses a lot, and he seemed to know his way around this one. He pet Absalom's nose, and then slipped the bridle over his head and secured it. For a few moments, Thad stood there petting Absalom's glossy neck, and then he led him toward the gate.

"This is a truly beautiful horse," Thad said.

Lydia opened the gate for him, and then shut and secured it when he and the horse were outside again.

"*Yah*, he is," Lydia agreed. "Now come on—the sleigh has lots of space in the back for your supplies. It doesn't lock, of course, and it isn't covered, so you'd want to make sure you put all your supplies inside overnight. No one in our community would steal from you, but there are Englishers who like to take advantage of our trusting ways, and I'd rather you didn't lose anything more in your stay here."

She led the way toward the sleigh, and Absalom followed Thad's lead easily enough. The horse loved to go out for a sleigh ride.

Lydia stopped in front of the sleigh. It seated four, two

in the front and two in the back where she imagined he'd put his tools. It was a beautifully carved wooden sleigh that her father had purchased from the buggy dealer over in Bird-in-Hand. He'd saved for it, and then the price was reduced mid-summer, and he'd purchased it. It said something that her father was willing to lend it. Or perhaps it said something about how much her family now owed Thad.

"This is the sleigh—and those are the traces. I'm sure you've seen a buggy hitched up before, and this is the same idea, but what you need to keep in mind is…"

And she outlined the steps of the process, how to hitch a horse up, how to avoid common mistakes, how to make sure the horse would be safe in bad weather.

And as she talked, Thad's blue gaze stayed locked on her with a rather sweet look on his face. Then he'd look over at the sleigh, then back to her, and she was reminded of the common proverb that said being listened to almost felt like being loved. She realized in a rather breathless rush that if Adel weren't quite so overwhelmed, and Thad were a proper Amish man, Lydia would sit down with their matchmaker and make a quiet request.

But Thad was Beachy Amish. It didn't matter if he was kind and sweet, and made her feel like blushing. But maybe one day soon *Gott* would provide her with a man very much like Thad Miller.

And then she'd make him the best donuts of his life, and be proud to do so.

Chapter Four

Thad tightened the last strap under Lydia's supervision, and he gave the horse a reassuring pat on the shoulder. Absalom shot him an annoyed look—as annoyed as a horse could manage—and shuffled his big hooves. Was he really going to finish out a week of work using a horse and sleigh? It did seem like the best option, especially considering the falling snow and his need to get out into the field, but this was far from the comfort of his pickup truck.

"Too tight?" Thad asked.

"No, it's good." Lydia put a finger under the leather strap and gave it a tug. "That's about right. Nicely done. Now you know how to hitch up a sleigh."

Thad certainly hoped he'd be able to repeat it alone, but he had a feeling that he could ask any Amish man around, and he'd get any help he needed. That was the nice side of the Old Order Amish communities. They were always happy to lend a hand, so Thad wasn't going to be exactly alone in this. But he was going to be personally responsible for this horse and sleigh. And the horse, gorgeous as he was, didn't look like he'd decided to like Thad yet.

"Anything I should know about Absalom here?" Thad asked.

"You know how to care for a horse, of course?" she asked.

"Of course." He cast her a smile.

At least in theory. He knew how much feed a horse this size needed, how much water, how to muck out a stall and brush him down. He could care for his hooves, too. This was his veterinarian experience; he'd never owned a horse of his own.

"Well, Absalom is a sweetheart," Lydia said. "Mostly."

The big horse shuffled his hooves again.

"And when he's not?" Thad asked, casting the horse a wary look.

"You just have to be firm," Lydia said. "I'm sure you'll be fine. Once he's pulling the sleigh, he's happy enough. It's just when he's waiting that he can get ornery. Keep him moving, I say."

Great. At least a temperamental truck didn't bite or kick. But he'd dealt with horses ill and in pain. He'd have to figure out how to manage this horse.

"You'll like the Draschel bed-and-breakfast. It's very comfortable," Lydia said. "They have lots of Englisher guests who stay, and they always get good reviews online."

She sounded casual enough chatting about online reviews.

"You...check online?" he asked.

"Claire does," Lydia replied. "At the library in Redemption. A librarian there helps her to look up their reviews. She gets five stars most of the time, and I've been told that's very good. The point is, you'll be comfortable."

"You think I need a little coddling, do you?" he asked with a laugh.

"Well…" Lydia's cheeks reddened. "I thought you might, truthfully. And Claire has batteries in the rooms so you can charge your cell phone."

Thad had been about to argue that he could handle Old Order comforts—or at the very least he'd been determined to in order to impress her—but that battery pack sounded very useful indeed. Even the Amish farmers who needed him would walk down to their closest phone hut and dial his cell phone number.

"I actually will need that," he said. "That's how people reach me."

"I thought so." She smiled. "Are you ready to head down to the B&B?"

"I am," he said.

"You're driving," she said, nodding at the sleigh. "I'll give you a quick driving lesson on the way down there."

Perhaps Thad had that coming. He shot her a grin. "Is this revenge?"

Lydia's smile faltered, and she quickly shook her head. "No, no. I would never do something to get revenge. That's wrong. That's—"

"I'm joking," he said, reaching out and touching her elbow. "Just joking. I hope I don't end up in a pothole."

She stilled, then swallowed hard. He'd touched her elbow. Right—he couldn't just casually touch her, could he? He pulled his hand back.

"Sorry," he murmured. "I hope I don't offend you, Lydia. For me, this is how I joke with my sister, so I truly don't mean any disrespect."

"Like your sister?" Her expression and her stance both relaxed.

"I have three of them," he replied.

"I'll try not to be so touchy about it, then," she said. "I suppose we'll both have to adjust to this little partnership, won't we? And you won't end up in a pothole. You'll stay on the road. Absalom is smarter than that. Two minds are better than one."

Even when one of those minds was a horse. She had a point there. Just then a tow truck crept down the drive and pulled to a stop beside Thad's silver pickup.

"Good timing," Thad said. "Let me just unload my supplies, get my truck on the way, and then you can give me those driving lessons."

About forty minutes later, after his truck was towed away and his supplies were all safely stowed in the back of the sleigh, Thad and Lydia got up into the front seat and Thad took the reins.

"You hold the reins like this—" Lydia pulled the reins through her hand in demonstration. "The left rein is on top, and the right rein comes through your middle and ring finger like so..."

Thad was somewhat familiar with this, just from observing his clients. When she handed him the reins, he put them through his fingers and Lydia leaned over and tugged the reins a bit tighter in his grip.

"Like that," she said.

She was close to him—so close that he could smell the scent of lavender from her hair. This certainly felt different to be on the receiving end of the driving lessons, and he felt a refreshed bit of sympathy for her earlier driving lessons in his truck.

"Now, to get Absalom to start moving, you relax the reins and give him some slack. He knows what that means, and you say, 'Let's go.'"

"Okay…" Thad did as she told him, relaxing his grip on the reins.

"More…" Lydia put a hand over his and pushed his hand forward a few more inches.

"Let's go," Thad said firmly.

Absalom started forward and the sleigh started to move with a little jerk, the runners slicing over the freshly fallen slow.

"There you are," Lydia said. "Nicely done."

Thad cast her an appreciative glance. Her cheeks were pink and her gaze was on the drive ahead of them.

"You're a good teacher," he said.

"Danke." Her gaze flickered in his direction. "Eyes on the road, Thad."

He chuckled and did as she told him, and they came up to the end of the drive.

"Now, let's stop here before we turn. Just tug gently on the reins and say 'Whoa,'" she said, her voice low and encouraging.

Thad tugged the reins and said, "Whoa, now…"

The horse came to a stop.

"Very good." Lydia touched his hand. "Pull back a little farther to keep him stopped…"

Thad was enjoying this—not just the chance to drive a horse-drawn sleigh, but also being taught by Lydia. She was a patient and encouraging teacher, he realized. Maybe he shouldn't have just walked away from her when he was showing her the ropes with driving his truck. He'd thought he was showing that he trusted her to be fine behind the wheel, but her teaching technique seemed to be better than his had been.

"Now, when you turn just tug the direction you want to turn," Lydia instructed. "This time, it's your right-hand rein—the bottom one. A gentle tug tells him the direction to turn, and you give a bit of slack—the right-hand rein less slack—and he'll start moving in the right direction. He's well trained so it doesn't take much, and the bit in his mouth is very sensitive. He can feel everything."

Thad gave the bottom rein a little tug and then gave some slack as she'd instructed, and Absalom started forward again in the right direction onto the road.

"This is a whole lot different than driving a truck," he said.

"*Yah*, I can attest to that," she replied.

Thad shot her a smile. "You're a better teacher than I am, Lydia. I'm sorry I didn't take more time to show you how things worked with the truck."

"It's all right," she replied. "I'm none the worse for wear. It's your truck that's damaged."

"Honestly, that could have happened even to a more experienced driver," he said.

The horse plodded along at a brisk pace, but it was still considerably slower than a gas vehicle moved. Thad settled back in the seat as they jingled down the road, the bells on Absalom's tack providing the cheery music. As they approached a stop sign, Lydia put a hand on his forearm and he reined Absalom in.

"Nice," she murmured.

Then he relaxed the reins and said, "Let's go…"

He was getting the hang of it, Thad thought, and it was a rather satisfying feeling to have control of a horse-drawn sleigh. It was an entirely different experience—a little more seat-of-his-pants, and more of a cooperation between man and horse.

"Do you…like this?" she asked hesitantly.

"Driving a sleigh?" he asked.

"Yah."

He chuckled. "I do like it. It's…a really different experience. I guess you can get used to anything, but I see the allure of horse-drawn vehicles."

"It's a nice thing that it takes more time to get places," she said. "In your truck, it would probably take five minutes to get to the B&B. But in a sleigh on the back roads, it's twenty minutes at least."

"Is the nice part more time with me?" Thad teased.

Her cheeks pinked. "More time to *think*, Thad. More time to prepare yourself, or to pray before you arrive somewhere."

"Right, of course."

She did have a point about slowing down the hustle and bustle of life. As a Beachy Amish man he didn't listen to the radio, but add to that quiet the slower pace with a horse, and he found his own mental circles slowing as well. It was calmer, and if he had any anxiety, it would drift away on a sleigh ride like this one.

"That's not to say that more time to talk with a friend isn't nice, too," she added after a beat or two of silence.

He cast her a rueful smile. "I agree."

Although this would slow down his workdays considerably, and he'd spend more time traveling to different farms and less time at the clinic. But he could make it work for a few days while his truck was being fixed.

With anyone else beside him, it might be a test of his patience, but with Lydia acting as his human map, he had a feeling he'd enjoy himself. He was reminded of Christmas songs about sleigh rides together.

As the miles slowly passed to the clop of horse's hooves, they came upon the green-on-white sign for the Draschel B&B. A two-story white house with a veranda out front and a *dawdie haus* built onto the side was set back from the road, visible through some snow-capped trees. It looked neat and welcoming, with some evergreen fans tied to the front of the veranda banister. He spotted a little boy perched within the branches of one of the trees in front of the house, snow filtering down from the branch he lounged on. At the base of the tree sat a German shepherd, sniffing around at the trampled snow.

Thad tugged on the reins, slowing Absalom, and then tugged a little harder on the right-hand rein to get Absalom to turn into the drive.

"Nicely executed turn, Thad," Lydia said, and Thad found himself enjoying the way she pitched her voice, low and private, just for him.

"Can I ask one thing?" Thad asked.

"Of course."

"Do they have an indoor bathroom or an outhouse here?"

"Indoor facilities," she replied.

And he felt a wave of relief. For the next few days, he'd be living Old Order Amish, and he wondered how he'd fare in Lydia's eyes. He hoped she'd watch him handling things just fine. When he left here, he didn't want to be "that Beachy Amish fellow who couldn't hack it."

"Hello!" Aaron Beiler called from his perch in the tree. He was a seven-year-old boy with a mop of unruly blond curls that poked out from under a little black hat, an imitation of the adult version. Aaron needed a new haircut, by Lydia's estimation, but his mother Claire would get to it. She had another little one—a baby girl named Esther—who needed her attention, too, besides running the B&B with her husband.

Lydia climbed out of the sleigh and shaded her eyes against the sun to make him out. He was in the broad, bare branches of a large oak tree at the far end of the yard.

"Hello, Aaron!" she called.

The side door opened then, and Claire appeared in the doorway with the baby on her hip. She waved at Lydia with a smile.

"Claire, I've brought a guest for you," Lydia said as she approached the steps. She glanced back at Thad, who'd headed over to tie up Absalom at the hitching post.

"Oh?" Claire said, but she did straighten a little. "That's good news, Lydia. We had a guest cancel. Who is he?"

"This is the veterinarian taking Dr. Ted's place while he's on leave. His name is Thad Miller. I'm helping him find the local farms until Dr. Ted gets back, and...well, it's a long story, Claire, but I ended up breaking his vehicle, and he's now borrowing our horse and sleigh for a few days until he gets his truck fixed."

"You broke it?" Claire's eyebrows rose in surprise.

"*Yah*, I did. I cannot lie about it. Anyway, he can't very well stay in a hotel in town with a sleigh, can he? So we suggested he come stay here."

"And he can drive a sleigh?" Claire asked. "He's an Englisher, I take it?"

"He's Beachy Amish."

The women exchanged a look that held volumes. Englishers could be forgiven many foibles, but the Beachy Amish were just a little too close to a "proper way of life," and a little too far away at the same time.

"And he can drive a sleigh as of today," Lydia added. "I just gave him his first lesson. Honestly, he'll need help with the horse and hitching. I was hoping Joel wouldn't mind."

"He won't mind a bit," Claire said. "Don't worry about that."

Claire cast her attention over Lydia's shoulder.

"We're happy to have you!" Claire said, raising her voice. "My name is Claire Beiler, and my husband and I run this establishment. Lydia says you'll be staying for a few days?"

Thad came up behind Lydia and he gave Claire a friendly smile.

"If you have the room for me, I'd be grateful," he said.

"Of course," Claire said. "We have a nice downstairs suite right off the kitchen. My family sleeps upstairs, so you'll have some privacy and some quiet. I have breakfast ready at eight o'clock sharp, but you can have cereal and baked goods if you need to get moving earlier. The price includes a hearty supper as well, but you'll need to fend for yourself at lunchtime, I'm afraid."

"That's perfectly fine," Thad said. "It sounds wonderful."

"Oh, there's my husband now," Claire said.

Joel Beiler was a slim man who walked with a pronounced limp, and he came out from the backyard. When he walked up, Thad put a hand out to shake, and Joel caught his hand with the wrong hand in an awkward greeting. His left arm was thinner and wasn't as cooperative—the result of a hereditary illness.

The men moved off together and started to chat, and Lydia reached out and touched Esther's plump cheek.

"Come in for some tea," Claire said.

"Oh, that reminds me," Lydia said, following her friend inside. "I was at Adel's place earlier, and she just seems... I don't know, sad. A little run down and despondent. My mother is rounding up some of us for a sunshine party. We want to go over after supper, about seven. Would you come, too?"

"Of course," Claire said. "I think I could get away once Esther has her bath. Joel can take care of things with the *kinner*. What's happening with Adel? Is it the baby blues?"

Lydia looked over her shoulder before Claire shut the door, and she saw Thad and Joel talking together, and Thad lifted his gaze just then and met hers. Her heart skipped a beat.

She quickly looked away as the door thumped closed. Beachy Amish or not, he was a handsome man.

"Lydia?" Claire said. "Is it the baby blues?"

Lydia took a deep breath, trying to shake off the man's effect on her heartbeat.

"Maybe," Lydia said. "I think she's just tired out.

She's been working so hard with matchmaking, and taking care of her own *kinner*, and having the new baby, plus the farm… It's a lot."

"It is a lot," Claire agreed. "Come have some tea and we'll discuss this sunshine party. Sounds like Adel needs it."

That evening, Lydia, her mother Willa, Claire Beiler, Delia Lehman, and Verna Lantz all packed up some items that Adel might find useful, and headed out to the Knussli farm in the bright, silvery moonlight of a cold, clear night. They had formed a sort of sisterhood among them of the women who owed Adel so much. The snow had stopped falling and the clouds cleared, revealing the brilliant full moon and a sky filled with stars as Lydia and Willa drove up to the house in their gray covered buggy.

There were three other buggies already parked outside the farmhouse, and Lydia guided their buggy into a spot at the end of the lineup. Light glowed merrily from the downstairs windows, and Lydia could hear the sound of laughter from inside as she collected one cloth bag that contained some little crocheted baby clothes and a few stuffed toys for Adel's little boy, and Willa collected a banana cake and a few other baked goods. Then they made their way to the side door.

The door popped open before they even got to the first step, revealing Verna's smiling face. She had her baby boy up on her shoulder, and her stepdaughter, Mandy, was at her side. The girl was about six now, and she had several missing teeth and a bright smile.

"We're all here now," Verna said, and she stepped back to let them in.

"Oh, let me hold him," Willa said. "I'll trade you baked goods for some time snuggling this little guy."

Verna chuckled and let Willa put down her basket and scoop the baby boy into her arms. For just a moment, Lydia felt a little surge of envy. She and Verna used to be two single women "of a certain age" in the community, and there had been some comfort in their shared single status. But Verna had gotten married, and she now had a husband, a stepdaughter, and a baby boy of her own. Verna had the life that Lydia longed for, and redirecting that envy into a prayer of thanks to *Gott* for having provided for her friend wasn't easy today. But she managed it.

Gott, *thank You for Verna's husband and* kinner. *And as You bless her, please remember me.*

The women were gathered in around the table. Adel sat with a plate piled high with treats in front of her. Her little boy played with a set of toy cows on his hands and knees on the floor. Delia had brought her stepdaughter Violet with her. Violet was as tall as Delia already, and at fourteen she was starting to fit in with the grown women. She was playing a hand-clapping game with Mandy, who stared at Violet with the adoration of a little girl for a teenager.

Claire hadn't brought the children with her tonight, as she'd already told Lydia, and she stood up to help Lydia and Verna put their offerings on the kitchen counter.

"My *mamm* made banana cake," Lydia said. "And I brought some crocheted toys for the *kinner,* and another blanket that will be big enough for your bed this winter."

"You are all being just too kind to me!" Adel said, and she pushed back her chair and came to give each of them a hug. "The only ones we're missing today are my sister, Naomi, and Sarai."

Naomi and her husband Mose lived in Indiana, and they had two *kinner* already—twin girls—and Sarai and her husband Arden were living in Ohio, and while they didn't have any *kinner* yet, everyone was expecting a letter announcing something any time now.

Lydia hugged Adel back.

"We're here for you today," Lydia said. "You're always working for everyone else, and it's time we took care of you. Where is Jake?"

"Jake is putting Samuel to bed," Adel said. "He'll probably stay up there and let us women visit. He doesn't get a lot of quiet reading time, so I think he'll enjoy it."

"If he's like any other young parent, he'll fall asleep before he gets the chance to crack that book open," Willa chuckled. "And no one will judge him."

"I didn't get my cleaning done before Claire and Delia showed up," Adel said.

"Perfect!" Lydia said, casting her friend a smile. "I see dishes in the sink. Claire and I can start on those, can't we, Claire?"

"Absolutely," Claire said, pushing back her chair. "By the time we leave, your floors will be mopped, your dishes will be done, and we'll have food in your pantry for the next few days."

"I'm normally the one planning sunshine parties," Adel said with a misty smile.

"And we've learned from you," Lydia said with a grin. "Go sit. We have this under control."

Lydia and Claire headed over to the kitchen sink and Lydia started the water. Claire leaned against the counter and gave Lydia a sly little smile.

"What?" Lydia asked, putting a squirt of dish soap into the water.

"That Thad Miller is a very nice man," Claire said. "He talked about you a lot after your *daet* picked you up. Lydia this and Lydia that…"

"Well, I was the only one he really spent much time with," Lydia said.

Claire shrugged. "He told a very funny story about you wrecking his truck. He felt terrible to put you into that situation at all. He had my husband in stitches, though."

"Laughing at me?" Lydia's stomach dropped. Had Thad been making fun of her?

"Not at you," Claire said. "At himself. He made himself look like an absolute fool in that story, and you came out of it looking like a queen."

"Oh…" That was oddly reassuring. He spoke well of her, even after she'd damaged his truck. It was nice to know that he was the same to her face as he was behind her back.

"Oh, and my cousin the bishop told me that the hospital in Greenberg has put out a request for toys for the *kinner* over Christmas," Claire said. "They sent a flyer in the mail about it."

"They need more toys?" Lydia asked.

"They do. And I'm sure they'll collect a lot of donations, but we thought of you. Zedechiah was going to go tell you about it himself, but I said I'd be seeing you tonight," Claire explained. "They have more children coming through the emergency rooms and admitted for illness over the holidays than ever before, and they wanted to have a small, comforting toy for each child. Nothing sharp or plastic."

"Something crocheted and stuffed, perhaps?" Lydia asked with a smile.

"*Yah*, I think that's their hope. I don't know if you'll have much time—"

"I'll make the time," Lydia said. "And I do have a few lambs and Noah's Arks set aside already."

"If you'd make the toys, we'll collect money to pay for the van to deliver them," Claire said.

"That would be very kind," Lydia replied. "And of course, I'll make the toys. I don't have *kinner* of my own to chase after. I have time."

Perhaps that was the hidden blessing of her life just as it was. She did have time to make toys for the sick *kinner* in the hospital, while the other women were bustling around getting ready for Christmas, for family visits, and running their own homes. If *Gott* needed her to make toys, then she would make toys.

The sink was now full of fluffy suds and hot water. Lydia turned the tap off and started putting dishes into the water.

"Lydia, tell us more about this Beachy Amish man you've been guiding around Redemption!" Delia called from the table. "Your *mamm* was just telling us about him."

Claire gave her a teasing little smile.

"Beachy Amish is the key description here," Lydia said with a laugh. "And I ruined his truck, so you can stop playing innocent. I know what you're thinking. He's

Beachy. We're Old Order. I've never known a single Beachy Amish to adopt our ways. Not one."

"There's always a first time," Willa said, her back to Lydia.

Lydia sighed. *Yah*, her parents would do their best to convert poor Thad to their Old Order ways. And they would fail.

Lydia was smarter than to get hopeful for a hopeless situation. Lydia wanted a husband, not a lost cause! Her romantic hopes hadn't gotten her anywhere in all this time. It was time to get practical. And right now, a hospital needed her crochet skills. It didn't get more practical than that.

Chapter Five

Thad listened closely to Joel Beiler as he gave the directions to get from the B&B back to the Speicher acreage and he committed them to memory. These snow-covered back gravel roads in Amish country could all blend together after a while, but the people who lived out here knew the area well. They described sagging old barns, stretches of oak trees, three-way stops and railroad tracks…it helped that they knew every family that lived in these farms and acreages for miles around.

"And they're on the left-hand side," Joel concluded. "You can't miss them."

"Danke," Thad said. "Much appreciated."

He'd done most of the hitching up on his own this morning. Joel stood there watching his progress, clearing his throat from time to time if Thad was about to do something wrong. But it was helpful all the same.

Once Thad was on the snowy road, he leaned back in the sleigh seat and felt a rush of freedom. Funny—he felt more alive and filled with possibility this morning than he had in literally years. Maybe it was the fresh air, or the slower pace of the horse, or just the sense of festive fun that came with a sleigh ride and those jingling bells, but Thad couldn't deny it. And Joel was right. After following the directions, he found that he recognized the road where the Speichers lived—at least Absalom did! The horse perked up and headed down the drive without any direction from Thad at all.

Lydia emerged from the door just as he pulled up. She hadn't brought that big carpet bag with her this time, he noticed. When he reined Absalom in, he felt a little bad for the horse. Poor guy thought he was coming home, but this was only a pit stop. Lydia gave the horse a quick look over, then got up into the sleigh next to him on the bench seat.

"Did you hitch up yourself?" she asked.

"I did. Joel oversaw it, though. No need to worry."

She chuckled. "Just checking."

Thad released the reins and gave them a little flick. He'd discovered that this worked just as well to get Absalom moving once more. The horse started forward again and he steered him in a circle and back up the drive toward the road.

"So this morning, we're heading to Nathan Lapp's farm to take a look at a sick calf," Thad said. "I looked at the map, but I can't tell where it's at."

"Don't worry. Take a left at the road," she said.

They turned onto the road, and for the next few minutes, they were focused on navigating a four-way stop and then some oncoming traffic. Being in a sleigh felt a whole lot more vulnerable than being surrounded with the steel of a pickup truck. There was very little that stood between him and the other vehicles, and he was very aware of that when a truck whipped past them.

Absalom didn't even flinch, though. He just plodded steadily on.

When they finally got into the clear, Thad exhaled a pent-up breath.

"You're doing fine," Lydia murmured.

He liked that she cast out reassurances like that. He needed it more than he realized. He wasn't used to needing instruction at this point in his life, and being inexperienced in something tipped his self-confidence off-balance.

"I'm not used to being the pupil anymore," Thad said.

"Ah, you're used to being the doctor," she said.

"I guess so," he agreed. "But I always worked really hard to be the guy who was most informed, who was most prepared. Even as a boy."

"Oh, dear. Did you not feel safe?"

That thought had never occurred to him before.

"No, nothing like that," he said. "I came from a loving home. I was just a boy who struggled with social connections. Making friends wasn't easy for me back then. I've learned a lot since then—I make friends more easily now—but back then I got tired of trying and decided that I would just be the guy who knew more, who achieved more."

"Who went on to veterinarian school," she said softly. "When the others stopped their schooling and probably settled down to get married."

That was a loaded observation, because she was right. His educational ambitions went against his community's ways of doing things. While it wasn't prohibited, his education certainly clashed with tradition. His Beachy Amish community stopped schooling after high school.

The Old Order Amish communities stopped after the eighth grade. So his career would go against Lydia's community, too, and maybe her sympathies, for all he knew.

"I know it sounds prideful," Thad said. "And maybe it was. I wanted to carve out my own niche, have something that was mine."

"Didn't you miss your friends and your community?" she asked.

"I did," he said. "But mostly, I was focused on what I wanted to achieve. I always said I'd go back and work as a vet in my own community."

"Did you do that?" she asked.

"No." No, as it turned out, his old schoolmates didn't miss him as much as he'd missed them. They had gotten married and started families. He had even less in common with them then. It had been an awkward imbalance—something he'd gotten used to in his social interactions. "It didn't work out that way. Their lives moved on, and my career moved on. In some ways, animals were easier than people."

"I find crochet much easier than dealing with people, too, sometimes. Crochet makes sense. I can learn it. People…are harder to learn."

Thad met her gaze and for a moment, he felt that mutual understanding passing between them. She understood this, didn't she? She'd be the first.

"Did it push you to be the best?" he asked. "In your crochet, maybe?"

She shook her head. "Not really. If you spend a lot of time by yourself working with yarn instead of getting married and starting your own family, you end up being rather good at your craft just because of the time you

put into it. So I'm known for my crochet work. I'm…
skilled. But I didn't aim for that."

They were opposites there. She had accidentally become the best at her craft, and he'd been driven to be the
best. It wasn't part of their culture or their belief system
to try to be better than anyone else, but there had been a
deeply rooted seed inside of Thad that had needed just
that. He still felt mildly uncomfortable about that fact.

"You seem so personable," he said. "You're very ap-
proachable. Very friendly."

"Danke," she said. "You seem like you get along with
people just fine now, too."

"I got better with age," he said, and he shot her a grin.
She chuckled in response.

He'd gotten more confident, too. That was the difference. With his education and his career, he knew beyond
a doubt that he was very good at something that mattered, and that had straightened his shoulders.

But sometimes when he was learning something new,
like driving a sleigh in Amish country, he felt catapulted
back to his college days when he was the fish out of
water both at home and at school—when no one understood him, and he derived a lot of company from his
studies. Or back to the days when he was a boy and his
cousins were roughhousing and having fun, and they
didn't try to include him. He'd just made sure that he
got better grades than they did. He'd taken a fierce personal pride in getting every question right in math. Fo-
cusing on the next step up had gotten him through some
lonesome times. He'd always thought that when he "arrived," he wouldn't feel lonely anymore. But it didn't
seem to work that way.

"We're going to turn right up here," Lydia said.

The Lapp farm was much like the other Amish farms. A white farmhouse sat at the front of the property, and beyond was a large chicken coop with an enclosed yard where a large flock of chickens was scratching and pecking, the snow not seeming to bother them in the least. Beyond that was a red barn, the stables, and then farther on another barn and pasture rolling out as far as Thad could see.

A boy sat on the front steps of the house, and when he spotted them, he jumped up and ran inside. He emerged a moment later and a man came to the door and looked out over his head. He was a portly man with a full married beard without the mustache, as was the Amish custom.

"That's Nathan Lapp," Lydia said. "And his son Jonathan."

Right… He could already feel the certainty that the sick calf belonged to the boy. Nathan came outside and waited until Thad got out of the sleigh. Nathan gave Lydia a nod of hello.

"Hi, I'm Thad Miller," he said in Pennsylvania Dutch. "I'm standing in for Dr. Ted."

He made his usual introductions and shook hands with Nathan, and Lydia went around and tied Absalom to the hitching post. He felt a flush of embarrassment that he hadn't done it himself.

"It's my calf that's sick," Jonathan spoke up. "I sit with her as long as I can during the day, but she's not getting better."

"I'll take a look at her and see what I can do," Thad said, and he pulled his bag out of the back of the sleigh and slung it over his shoulder. His mind was already clicking ahead to the common ailments that occurred to calves.

"I take good care of her," Jonathan went on. "I keep her stall clean, and I give her fresh milk and I take her out into the pasture. I feed her the best hay, too. She was a tiny baby, and my uncle gave her to me for free because he said she was too little. But she was so cute and I even fed her with a bottle for three whole weeks. She drinks out of a bucket now."

"Jonathan," Nathan said quietly, and he laid a hand on the boy's shoulder.

The boy fell silent and took a step back, but when Thad looked over at him, the boy was watching him with such pleading in those big, brown eyes that it gave Thad's heart a tug. This boy loved his calf, and if Thad could help this little heifer, he would. It was too close to Christmas for young Jonathan to have his heart broken.

Lydia followed Nathan and Thad, who walked ahead, and Jonathan fell in next to her as they tramped through the snow. The boy walked resolutely, his shoulders straight and marching along in perfect imitation of his father. Lydia had to smile. His black felt hat was pushed down low on his head.

"Is he any good?" Jonathan asked Lydia. Again, that imitation of a man's cadence of speech. Trying to be so grown up.

"Who? Thad?" Lydia asked.

"*Yah.* Is he a good vet? Because my calf needs a really good one." There was a crack in his ever-so-grown-up voice, and the little boy shone through.

"Well, from what I've seen so far, he is a very good vet," she replied gently.

The boy nodded. "I'm praying for my calf, you know. Her name is Bobli, because I fed her with a bottle like a little *bobli* when we first got her."

"That's a cute name. And I'm glad you're praying for her," she said. "*Gott* cares for your calf, too, Jonathan."

"Will you pray for my calf, too?" Jonathan asked. "Just an extra prayer or two. It might help."

"Of course I will."

"*Danke.* My *mamm* is praying, too, and I've noticed that *Gott* seems to answer her prayers. She tells us about it. But she says I can't get my hopes up, because sometimes *Gott* says no. But how could *Gott* say no about a little calf?"

And what would they do if Jonathan had to face his first no from *Gott*? Life could be painful, too. She put a hand on his shoulder.

"We'll just keep praying, okay?" she said.

They arrived at the barn, and Lydia spotted the calf's stall right away because there was a gray horse blanket on top of the small animal. She lay in a fresh bed of hay, eyes shut. But Lydia could make out the rise and fall of the animal's side through the blanket—she was asleep. When the door banged shut, the calf's eyes opened.

Thad squatted down next to the animal, and with tender care, he lifted the blanket. He looked in the calf's eyes, and opened her mouth. He checked her temperature with a battery-operated thermometer and took a sample of her saliva. He felt her limbs with careful squeezing, and then went around and got a sample of her droppings, too.

"It looks like she has a virus," Thad said. "I'll have to do some tests to see exactly what she's got, but to start out, I'm going to give you some powder to add to her milk. It'll help with her upset stomach and should settle that down and make her more comfortable."

Thad's glance landed on Lydia and she saw the regret shining in his eyes. This calf was not in good shape, but Jonathan squeezed into the stall next to the animal now, petting her head and crooning to her.

Thad came over to stand next to Lydia, but his words were meant for Nathan who stood a couple of feet away.

"It doesn't look good," Thad said.

"I didn't think so," Nathan said. "Can anything be done?"

"I'm going to give her a shot of an antibiotic to help if there is any secondary infection," Thad said.

"How much will that cost?"

"It's not bad." He told him the price.

"All right… I suppose we can do that," Nathan replied.

"And keep her warm. I'll see if I can narrow down what's affecting her, but the antibiotic is the best I can do at present. Then, of course, there is the medication to settle her stomach—that will make her sleepy, too, so don't worry if she sleeps a lot after you give it to her."

"And how much will that cost?" Nathan asked.

"I'll throw that in for free."

Nathan just nodded, and Thad administered the injection and shouldered his bag again. Thad shook young Jonathan's hand and then the adults headed back out of the barn, leaving Jonathan with his calf. The three of them walked back toward the house and the sleigh, and

Lydia felt a weight of sadness descend onto her like a heavy blanket.

"I shouldn't have taken the calf," Nathan said. "I can't use up all our money on one calf. We've got other animals to care for, and my son seems too attached to this one."

"He said he fed the calf by bottle," Lydia said. "That builds a bond."

"*Yah*, I know..." Nathan pressed his lips together and didn't say anything else.

When they got back to the sleigh, Thad left a small container of medication as well as a bill with Nathan. Then Lydia got back up into the buggy and waited while Thad untied the horse, backed him up by hand, and circled back around to get into the driver's seat. Thad was looking much more comfortable with reins in his hands now, and she watched as the leather strap slipped through his fingers and he gave a light flick. He'd caught on quickly, and she found herself looking at his strong, confident hands. Absalom started forward and they circled with the soft scrape of gravel poking through the snow against the sleigh's runners, and she tore her gaze away from him.

"This boy is very attached to his calf," Thad said.

"He asked me to pray for her."

Thad pressed his lips together. "He's a nice boy. I wish his calf were a little stronger, that's all." He was silent for a moment. "It wasn't a calf when I was his age. It was a dog. That dog was my very best friend. I used to look forward to coming home to him. I'd play with him, and we'd sit on the porch together, and I'd unload all of my trials from the day... I lost him when I was about Jonathan's age. It crushed me."

"I'm sorry, Thad," she said softly.

"It was a long time ago," he said. "But I know how much an animal can mean to a boy, and seeing how much he loves that calf, I just worry that Nathan isn't going to understand."

"You're a vet," she said. "You understand farm animals. They aren't pets."

"No, they aren't, but they still rely on people for absolutely everything," Thad replied. "Nathan seems very concerned about the cost of getting this calf healthy."

"Can you get her healthy?" she asked.

"I can try. Whether or not they should have taken on a premature calf isn't the point. They did."

Lydia didn't know Nathan very well. He was about ten years older than she was, so they weren't friendly. Besides, he was married, and while Lydia knew Nathan's wife, she was older than Lydia and therefore not exactly a pal, either. What kind of parents were they? They had well-behaved *kinner*. She knew that much. But would Nathan understand Jonathan's deep love for a calf they shouldn't have kept?

"They're good people," she countered.

"Their son will remember how they dealt with this," Thad said, and she could hear the restrained judgment in his voice. "It's not me they'll have to convince. It's Jonathan."

But the Lapps were good people, Lydia was sure of it, and she couldn't help but wonder how Thad really saw the Old Order Amish. Did he think they were cruel? Heartless? Backward? Because they weren't. And sometimes *kinner* had to learn lessons about sick animals and a family's financial budget.

"Would Beachy Amish do things differently?" Lydia could hear the tightness in her own voice.

"I'm sorry," Thad said. "I don't mean to offend you."

"But you think we Old Order are cruel, somehow," she said.

Thad cast her an apologetic look. "I didn't mean that. I'm just seeing a boy who loves an animal, and a man who is more concerned about the cost of veterinarian care than he is about his son's heart. He could have shown more compassion to his son."

"They'll talk in private," Lydia said. "Don't think that what you see as an outsider is the whole story, either."

There was always more to a story, always more to a relationship. And while she knew that Thad was coming to conclusions about their community, judgment went both ways. And judgment was never fair.

When they finished their calls that morning, Thad drove Lydia back home. As they came into the drive, she saw her brother's blue SUV parked next to the family buggy. Lydia instinctively looked toward the house. She could see the kerosene light lit in the kitchen.

"An Englisher visiting?" Thad asked.

"My Englisher brother," she replied. "Paul."

Thad leaned forward, getting a better look at the SUV. "How does your *daet* react to that?"

"My *daet* loves his son!" she said defensively. "It's like Nathan and Jonathan. They have a special relationship, but you won't see that from the outside."

"Lydia, I'm sorry about what I said earlier," Thad said with a sigh. "I know your family loves each other."

Lydia sighed. "We are quite the same, at heart. We just live more simply."

"I know that," Thad said.

Lydia looked toward the house, and her heart squeezed.

"They argue a lot," Lydia admitted. "My parents feel betrayed by my brother leaving like he did. I shouldn't be telling you that, but it's true. My *daet* thinks he should come home and live sensibly Amish, but Paul is married to an Englisher woman and his *kinner* have all been raised outside the Amish faith. His son came to stay with us last summer after he was getting into some trouble at school. So Paul has been part of things."

"And his wife?" Thad turned to look at her.

"Less so." Lydia winced. "Janet is nice. I like her. But she doesn't feel comfortable. We all talk in Pennsylvania Dutch and my parents try to convince her to become Amish. It's…awkward. My brother tends to come see us on his own. Sometimes he brings Janet with him, but not often."

Thad nodded. "It's hard for him."

"Very." And Lydia had seen what marriage was like when there wasn't unity in faith and family. It wasn't pleasant, and it was a confirmation of her own choices to make sure she married a good Amish man.

"*Danke* for helping me today," he said.

"My pleasure." Her gaze caught his and he returned her smile. "Tomorrow is Service Sunday. I know you think we're quite different from you—and maybe our worship is different—but I think you'll see that we're just people."

"Lydia—" he started.

"Will you come?" she interrupted him. "I think it

would do you good to see the community together. I can be your guide. And you understand the language, so you won't be left out. What do you say?"

"Are you sure you want me there?" Thad asked with a faint smile.

"Of course I do," she said. "I'd…" She swallowed. "I'd really like it."

"Then I'll come," he said.

She felt the smile touch her lips. "You could meet us here tomorrow morning. We'll be taking main roads and they're plowed. The sleigh won't work there. Come by at eight, and we'll get you to service one way or another."

He nodded. "All right. I'll be here."

When Lydia got out of the sleigh, she spotted her brother leaning against the doorjamb, watching her. She felt some heat in her face. She hadn't realized anyone had been watching.

Thad took the sleigh around and Lydia headed toward her brother.

"Hello, Paul," she said.

Paul stepped outside instead of letting her in. He looked tired. There were lines around his eyes and his shoulders were slumped forward. Paul was seven years older than she was, and he had a touch of gray in his rusty blond hair now, and he wore a golden wedding ring instead of a married beard. He was clean shaven. Somehow, that clean-shaven face made him seem more like the brother she'd grown up with.

"How long have you been here?" she asked.

"About half an hour," he said. "Long enough for *Daet* to lay into me."

"I'm sorry." She grimaced.

"Is that the Beachy Amish veterinarian?" he asked, jutting his chin toward the receding sleigh.

"*Yah*, that's him."

"He seems to like you," Paul said.

"I'm likable, Paul," she retorted, and her brother shot her a grin.

"I know, I know," he said. "I'm just saying that from a male perspective, he really likes you. As a woman. He's…attracted to you."

Was he? The thought that Thad might be seeing her as more than just a guide was both a little surprising and oddly thrilling.

"You could tell all that from a conversation in a sleigh?" she asked.

"*Yah*."

"Oh." She kicked her boot against the step. "I don't get that very often, you know."

"You could, Lydia," Paul said. "I keep telling you that there is a whole world out there. There are nice guys who'd be happy to meet you. There are jobs you could do, and people you can meet, and—"

"I'm Amish, Paul," she said firmly.

Paul pressed his lips together.

"And so were you," she added.

"Don't start where *Daet* left off," he replied. "You know I completely understand where you're coming from. But I'm looking at my sister who is living at home, no boyfriend, no suitor, and you could have a really full life if you just stepped outside of this world. You could be married and have those *kinner* you long for. You could have it all. I hate to see you just sitting at home with *Mamm* and *Daet*."

Lydia felt her annoyance start to rise. "You always think I have this pathetic life, but I don't. I have friends and family. I have nieces and nephews who need me. I have my charity work, too. A husband is not everything, Paul! If I leave, I'm shunned. I give up *everyone*."

"You'd have me and Janet," he said. "But I know. I left before I was baptized, so it's different for me. But you know that *Mamm* and *Daet* have a choice, too. They can just not tell people they saw you."

"You know our parents wouldn't lie. And I want more than hidden visits with my parents. I want my parents in my life. I want my community. You can't fill that gap on your own."

"But it's nuts, you know," he countered. "They don't have to do as they're told. They can choose their daughter." Paul sighed, then scrubbed a hand through his hair. "I don't want to argue about that. I get it. And I can't change how the church works, no matter how much I disagree with it. All I'm saying is, holed up here with *Mamm* and *Daet*, it doesn't seem like the family you want is coming together for you. And there are other Amish groups that are less rigid."

"Like the Beachys," she said softly. Like Thad, and his family with their dangerous liberalities mingled with familiar Amish beliefs.

"Like the Beachys," her brother agreed. "It's worth thinking about."

No, it wasn't. What was good for Paul was not good for her, and while she knew her brother loved her, he didn't see the life she valued so deeply. She wasn't a teenager needing advice. She was a grown woman who had given her vow to her church.

"I'm Old Order Amish, Paul," she said. "I believe in *our* way of life."

"Okay," Paul said, and he gave her an apologetic look. "I didn't mean to come across as so judgmental. I'm just trying to look out for you. You deserve a husband and kids, too."

"I'm just fine, Paul," Lydia said. "I'm happy."

And she was. Happiness did not depend upon circumstances—it was a choice. And Lydia had chosen happiness a long time ago. She'd found her place to contribute here, even without a husband. Everyone needed help sometimes, and that was where Lydia stepped in.

"I won't say anything else," her brother said. "I've said it and I'm done."

The door opened behind them and *Mamm* appeared in the doorway.

"There you two are," she said. "Come inside, would you? It's freezing out there. I've got pie, and Paul, your *Daet* loves you. He's just missing his son. Okay? Come back in."

It would be another family evening with Paul home, and Lydia cast her brother a smile. The evening would be somewhat tense, but it would also be nice to just have him in the kitchen again. They'd visit, *Mamm* would get to feed her son, and Lydia would crochet while she listened to them chat. There were sick *kinner* who needed cheering this Christmas, and Lydia had important work of her own to do. A husband was *not* everything.

She searched around inside of herself for more certainty of that. What if she never married? Would she look back on these choices and regret them?

But no one could see the future. All they could do was take the next right step and trust the rest to *Gott*.

Paul headed back up the stairs, and Lydia looked over her shoulder in the direction Thad had driven off. Her brother had said that Thad seemed to like her in a romantic sense, and that thought gave her a tickle through her middle. It didn't matter, and it wouldn't change anything, but it was a thought she'd tuck away and pull out again when she could be alone to relish it.

A handsome man like Thad thinking of her that way… It sent goosebumps up her arms underneath her coat. Maybe she had some hope of one day marrying after all, but she would not leave her faith to do it.

Chapter Six

The next morning, Thad arrived at the Speicher home just as Art and Willa were loading up some food into the back of their buggy. Art carried a big box and slid it into the back, and Willa added a bag stuffed full of something he couldn't make out. He knew that the Amish ate a meal together after the service, so maybe it was food to contribute. The sun was shining bright and golden, sparkling off the clean blanket of snow.

He reined by the stable, and Art came over and gave Absalom an affectionate pet. The older man was dressed all in black from his felt hat down to his polished black church boots. His gray beard fanned out over the front of his woolen overcoat, and he even had a knitted black scarf around his neck—proof that a woman cared for his comfort. Was it made by Lydia? Thad found himself wondering.

"How's he doing for you?" Art asked, stroking the horse's neck.

Thad tied the reins off and climbed out. He was getting a lot more comfortable with driving a sleigh now, and he was proud of his own progress. This was a new skill, all right, and he was looking forward to telling his parents about it. They'd be impressed.

Thad had done his best to dress for Service Sunday, but he knew he looked a far sight different from Art. He'd worn his own black wool coat, but his shirt was off-white, and his pants were dress pants, not the Old Amish broadfall style. But he did blend in better than he had before, and for that he felt a little bit victorious. He'd tried.

"Absalom is doing really well," Thad said. "He's a strong horse, and he's got faster instincts on the road than I do sometimes. I'm grateful that you've lent him to me."

"A good horse is smarter than his driver half the time," Art replied. "I'm glad he's doing well."

The horse missed home, though. Every time they got moving down the road that led to Absalom's home stable, the horse perked up and sped up his trot. Even animals knew where they belonged and knew where their comfort was. Absalom nuzzled Art's pockets and the older man spread his hands to show him he didn't have any treats. Absalom looked away, and Thad could almost feel the animal's wounded sense of justice.

"I have an extra courting buggy," Art said, then immediately gave Thad a flat look as if he could read Thad's mind. "Don't be getting any ideas, now. It's just an open top two-seater, and that's what we call it. You can drive that to church. We'll hitch Absalom up, and you'll do fine."

Thad had to admit, the term *courting buggy* had given him a little spark of interest. He could never actually court Lydia, but he wouldn't mind a little taste of what it might be like…

"I really appreciate that," Thad said. "You are really being incredibly kind to me."

"My daughter did break your fancy truck," Art said, and the word *fancy* came out dripping with disdain.

"I don't blame her at all," Thad insisted. "And I truly appreciate your kindness."

Art grunted and moved around to give his horse an affectionate pet.

"I don't think *Gott* ever intended for us to move so quickly as you all do in your automobiles," Art said. "Just because something is possible doesn't make it wise. It's possible to jump into a lake, but there are times of year that it's downright deadly."

"I actually have enjoyed the slower pace," Thad admitted. "At first I was impatient to get to my destination, but I'm learning to enjoy the journey."

With Lydia by his side…she was part of this experience for him, but he wouldn't tell her father that. Art would not appreciate that detail.

"*Yah*, well, there is wisdom to our way of life," Art said, giving the horse one last pat. "You'll see that in our service today, too. We might take things slowly, but there's depth and meaning in the slower pace."

"I appreciate the invitation to come along," Thad replied.

The invitation had come from his daughter, but Art gave a nod in acceptance, all the same.

"Why doesn't Lydia drive with you to service?" Art asked. "She can show you the way, and maybe give you a few pointers about driving a buggy versus a sleigh. That way you've got your own buggy for when you want to leave, too. My wife told me that I cannot expect you to stay the whole day. So… I'm not expecting that of you."

The older man fixed him with an arch look that Thad

wasn't sure how to interpret. Was he proud of himself for being open-minded, or was he hoping that Thad would reassure him that he'd stay just as long as everyone else?

"That's…considerate of you," Thad said. "I'd be glad to have Lydia show me the way."

That seemed like the safest answer.

"All right, then," Art said. "Let's get you hitched up."

After they'd hitched Absalom to the courting buggy, Lydia came out of the house last, another bag over her shoulder. She was dressed in a plum-colored cape dress with a thick black shawl wrapped around her body. She looked so modest, and so very feminine, he realized. She had a black bonnet on, too, shielding her face from view. Her mother was dressed in a similarly colored dress, but it was a little bit lighter, and her shawl looked a little more worn than Lydia's. But mother and daughter looked enough alike that Thad thought he could see a glimpse of what Lydia would look like in thirty years.

Lydia spotted Thad and shot him a sweet smile. Art met his daughter on the steps, accepted the bag from her, and said something that Thad couldn't hear. Lydia's eyes snapped toward Thad again, her glittering dark gaze resting gently on him for a moment, and then she nodded and headed in his direction.

"I'll be showing you the way, then?" Lydia asked, looking up at him in his buggy seat.

"*Yah*, if you're willing," he replied. "I haven't driven a buggy yet, either."

"You'll be fine," she said. "It works the same way. It's just a bit faster. A small buggy like this turns on a dime, where the sleigh needs more space to get around. That's about all."

"I'll still feel better with my teacher next to me," he said.

Lydia hoisted herself up and settled in next to him. The courting buggy was small enough that her arm pressed up against his, and his leg rested against hers. It was a little warmer snuggled up together like this, but he was very aware of her father just ahead. He'd better not appear to be enjoying this close proximity too much, or Art might change places with his daughter and he'd find himself plastered up next to a grumpy old man.

He stole a look at Lydia, and her cheeks were reddened already. She licked her lips and dropped her gaze. This did feel awfully cozy, and he noticed how close her hand was to his…close enough that he could take her hand if he was so inclined. Courting buggy was an excellent description for this little vehicle, it would seem.

Thad watched as Lydia's parents put the last bag into the back of the buggy and got up into their seats, too. Then the big, black buggy started forward, and Thad eased off the reins. This courting buggy felt different than the sleigh—he was higher off the ground, and the vehicle was a little faster. There was no friction against the snow to slow them down. He didn't need to say a thing, or flick the reins. Absalom immediately fell into pace behind the Speicher buggy ahead of them, plodding up the drive.

"I hope my *daet* wasn't preaching at you," Lydia said.

"What makes you think he was?" Thad asked, shooting her a teasing smile.

"I know my *daet*," she replied. "And he's introduced you into his list of people he's praying for during family worship."

"Me?" Thad felt a little touched. "What's he praying for?" Although he could probably guess.

"The same thing he prays for the grocery store manager, and the man who runs the hotel in town, and the Englisher woman who goes for a run down our road in those too-tight shorts..."

"I'm lumped in with all of them?" he asked.

She shrugged. "He prays that *Gott* will show you the light, and that you'll come to our faith."

"Ah." He understood the sentiment. He had a father who prayed just the same for people in their community, but it was odd to be on the receiving end of prayers for his literal soul.

"I'm sorry. Maybe I shouldn't have told you that," she said. "But he means well."

"No, it's okay," Thad replied. "I have a father very much like him. He's currently praying for our neighbors, too."

Lydia cast him a smile.

"You must live at home with them, then," she said. "Praying as a family."

He couldn't help the smile that tickled his lips. She was fishing. "No, I have my own place."

"But you're not married," she said. "What would people think?"

"No, I'm not married," he agreed. "But... I'm my own man."

"We don't do that here," Lydia said, shaking her head. "We stay home and help our parents until we've got a family of our own. It's only right to help them."

"It's a kind thing to do, but eventually you have to have your own space," Thad said. "I can still help and live on my own."

"And no one thinks you're worse for it?" she asked.

"No." A man getting his own place was simply how things worked. It was part of growing up, part of being ready to provide for his own wife when he met the right woman.

Lydia shook her head. "My brother said something like that about getting my own space, although if I did what he wants me to do, I'd be shunned. He thinks I'm wasting my life here with my *mamm* and *daet*."

"I didn't say that!" Thad said.

"He did." She turned her attention out the side of the buggy. He tried to get a glimpse of her face, but he could only see her black bonnet that shielded her from view.

"Your brother wants you to leave the faith?" Thad asked.

"*Yah.* He says I'd be happier. He thinks I'll stay single if I stay here."

"What do you think about that?" Thad asked.

"I'm Amish," she said, and turned then, her flashing gaze clashing with his. "I'm not going to be happier leaving everything I love behind, or abandoning my faith. I don't live a plain life because it's easier. It's harder in every way, and maybe it's harder for me to find a husband, too. But I'm following my conscience and living the way I believe *Gott* wants me to live."

"That's fair," he said. "It's noble, even."

She was very clear about where she stood, and he admired that. It was an attractive quality, although it was a quality that would disqualify the likes of him from getting a chance with her.

"The last time I saw my sister-in-law, Janet, she asked

me if I'd regret staying in the Old Order church if I never did marry and have *kinner* of my own," she said quietly.

"And?" he asked cautiously.

"I wouldn't regret staying in the church," she said, "but I'd be disappointed, of course, if I missed out on those blessings."

Lydia blinked and dropped her gaze, turning forward again. He'd seen the emotion in her dark eyes, though, and something deep inside of him rose up to meet her. She wanted a man to recognize what a truly amazing woman she was—and he *could*!

If only I could be her answer.

The thought had skimmed through his mind so quickly that he hadn't had time to quash it. He couldn't be her answer, he knew. He was Beachy Amish, and she was Old Order. Despite similarities, they came from different worlds. But sitting in the buggy on a chilly winter morning, he found himself wishing he could be the one to fill her heart and earn a place by her side.

Gott, please provide for her, he prayed in his heart. *And make her happy.*

It was a small, selfish part of his heart that stopped him from asking *Gott* to give her another man who saw the value in her like he did, because the thought of another man sitting next to her like this stung in a way that it shouldn't. It was just too hard to pray—at least in the moment. Give him time to talk himself into a more altruistic mindset. But *Gott* was good, and He wasn't hindered by Thad's petty jealousy.

May *Gott* provide for him, too.

Ahead of them, the Speicher buggy turned into a driveway that had a big, bold sign that read Swarey

Flowers. They turned in after it. As they rolled down the drive, Thad could hear the sound of laughing children, and a woman walked briskly past with a toddler in a snowsuit in her arms. More people came into view—groups of chatting men, women with identical thick black shawls covering them from the cold who disappeared into the farmhouse. A nearby pasture was filled with parked gray-topped buggies lined up in neat rows, their horses unhitched and in a corralled area with a filled feeder.

He glanced over at Lydia and she shot him a smile. She looked more relaxed now, and there was a sparkle in her eyes and a flush to her cheeks from the cold wind, and he was struck with just how lovely she was when she was happy. And here with her own people, Lydia was obviously happy.

"We're here," she said. "Welcome to Service Sunday."

Lydia noticed some of the women looking twice as she and Thad drove past and into the snowy buggy parking field. There was no top to this buggy to shield them from view, and new romantic connections were a constant source of good-willed gossip. She knew she'd be asked about this ride to service by several well-meaning friends. But Thad was ever so Beachy—he looked it this morning, too. His hat, his shirt that was store-bought and not the right style at all, and his pants that weren't broadfall, either. He looked like a man who was pretending to be Amish, even from a distance.

Still, it was nice to sit next to him this way. She hadn't ever been driven to church by a handsome man before, and it was certainly a thrill. He felt so solid and strong next to her, and today she wouldn't mind the gossip very much. Everyone would be set straight soon enough, but it might be nice to have people considering her as someone's sweetheart, even for a little while. The men here didn't seem to see her as a romantic possibility, but Thad liked her. He thought she was...*regal*. That was the word he'd used. She'd tuck that little compliment away for the rest of her life.

Lydia's parents parked their buggy in the field ahead of them. Her father went to unhitch the horse, and her mother went around to the back of the buggy to pull out the food she'd brought to contribute to the lunch the community would share after service.

Thad pulled in next to her parents' buggy, and she was impressed with how straight he parked the buggy. He had a knack for buggy driving. It was a necessary skill around here.

"That's a good parking job," Lydia said.

Thad grinned. "I'm improving."

"You are, for sure and certain," she said.

Her father was already leading the horse to the corralled-off area where the other horses were feeding.

"When my nephew Liam—that's Paul's son—came to stay with us last summer," Lydia said, "we tried to teach him how to drive the buggy. He never did get the feel for it."

"No?" Thad was silent for a moment. "I should be glad I'm picking it up, then."

"You should be."

Her father came striding back from the corralled area, and Lydia suddenly realized she was just sitting in the buggy next to Thad as if she had any right to it. Embarrassment heated her face. She quickly jumped down and smoothed her skirt with a shake. The untrodden snow was ankle deep out here, and it glistened in the morning sunlight.

"I'll help carry the food," Lydia said.

"No, no," Art replied. "I'll help your *mamm* carry it in. You just make sure Absalom is settled."

Her father looked toward his horse. She knew how much *Daet* loved his big draft horse, and that had been a testament to his generosity when he allowed Absalom to go with Thad for a few days. But he'd always want to make sure the horse was well cared for.

"Of course," Lydia said, and she exchanged an understanding look with her father.

Art walked briskly past and hoisted a box out of the back of the buggy. Thad headed over to Absalom and started to undo the first straps to unhitch the horse from the shafts.

"We've got it, Lydia," Willa said, grabbing the bags. "See you in there."

Lydia watched her parents as they headed across the snow in the direction of the farmhouse. If Thad was any other man, they'd be insisting that she be cautious about appearances, but it seemed that they weren't worried about those things with Thad Miller. Maybe they just saw a Beachy Amish veterinarian, or maybe it was the bishop's personal request that she help the man that eased their worries.

She looked back over to where Thad was unhitching, and she realized that she wasn't seeing a Beachy Amish veterinarian anymore. She was seeing a man she had grown to like.

Lydia headed over to where Thad stood to help him with the last of the unhitching. He put the tack across the seat of the buggy and came back to lead Absalom toward the corral. Absalom eyed Thad with a sparky look in his eye as Thad took the bit out of Absalom's mouth. He wasn't quick enough with the bridle, though, and before Lydia could even warn him, Absalom nipped at him with those big, sharp teeth.

Thad jumped, shut his eyes in a wince, and then looked at his hand. He gave it a shake and slid the bridle over Absalom's muzzle.

"Let's get you in there," Thad muttered.

"Absalom, that was very naughty of you!" Lydia reprimanded. "Did he get you, Thad?"

"Yeah, he got me," Thad said, and his voice was a bit tight, but he led Absalom toward the corral. Lydia hurried on ahead and opened the metal gate to the temporary enclosure. Absalom went inside, but he cast a look over his shoulder as he went. That horse was in a mood today!

"Are you all right?" she asked, turning back. Thad pulled off his glove and that was when she saw the blood. "Thad!"

"I don't know how bad it is," Thad said, "but it hurts, all right."

"I don't know what is with that horse today!" she said irritably, grabbing Thad's wrist and holding his hand up to get a better look. The horse's teeth had nipped the flesh along the side of his finger, and it was bleeding freely, but it didn't look too deep.

"I know what's wrong with him," Thad said. "We keep coming back to your place and he thinks he's coming home…but he never quite makes it back to his own stall."

Lydia looked back at Absalom. His eyes had that wicked look about them, though. Was that the horse's problem, homesickness?

Thad looked closer at his hand. "I could get away without stitches, I think."

He'd know—he was the one with some medical background.

"Come on," Lydia said. "Let's get you back to the house. There will be some bandages and salve and I'll get you fixed up."

"A Band-Aid should do it," Thad said, but he allowed her to lead him by the wrist. She held his hand out so that any dripping blood wouldn't get on their church clothes, and somehow his thick, strong wrist felt rather nice.

"That would be one big Band-Aid," she said ruefully. "No need to be overly brave, Thad. You know as well as I do, if you get an infection you'll be in trouble."

"You're making me look like a wimp," Thad chuckled, and he pulled his hand back, but he did slow his stride so that he stayed next to her.

"It must hurt," she said.

"This isn't the first time I've been nipped by a horse. I do work with sick and hurt animals, so this is part of the job."

A lesser man might have shouted at Absalom, or struck out at the horse in retaliation, Lydia realized. But Thad hadn't done that.

Some other families were arriving as they made their way back to the house, and Lydia absently waved to Verna and Adam Lantz as they pulled in. Verna was a good friend who had just recently married. She had her new baby boy in her arms, and their six-year-old daughter sat between them.

Verna leaned forward, a delighted look on her face, and Lydia hurried Thad along. *Yah*, she already knew her friends were intrigued with Thad.

At an Amish farmhouse, the front door was for salesmen, and the side door was for anyone who belonged there. So they headed up the side. The door opened and Adel Knussli appeared. She had the baby on her hip and her eyes widened when she saw Thad's hand.

"What happened?" Adel asked, backing up to let them inside. Several women were in the kitchen, including Willa, who was unpacking the food she'd brought. Lydia's father was nowhere to be seen, so he was probably out catching up with the men already.

"Our horse bit him," Lydia replied to Adel's question.

"Absalom bit him?" Willa asked across the kitchen. She planted her hands on her hips. "That naughty horse!"

"That's what I said," Lydia replied.

"We've got bandages," Delia said. "Violet—can you find that tin of bandages for me?"

Delia's stepdaughter, Violet, was a big help in the hosting duties. Delia's teenaged sons were probably outside with their step*daet* Elias setting up benches for the service and doing the outdoor work that came with hosting Service Sunday. Violet got a step stool and climbed up to reach an old cookie tin from a high cupboard. She brought it over to Lydia.

"Sit there," Lydia said, pointing to a chair by the window. Thad did as she asked him and slid into the chair. A drop of blood fell to the floor, and Delia passed over a clean rag. Thad wrapped it around his finger and squeezed hard so that his knuckles turned white. When he released it, the bleeding had slowed, and she could see the bruised and damaged flesh.

Lydia pulled up a chair and she positioned Thad's hand on his own knee so that she could work on him. First she used some disinfectant, wincing as she dripped it over the wound. She knew it would hurt, but the only sign Thad gave was a quick inhale of breath.

Then she tore open a package of sterile gauze and pressed it over the wound, and then taped it down with some medical tape. When he flexed his hand, the tape came loose, though, and she pulled it off.

"Stop doing that, Thad," she said. "You'll just have to be careful with that hand for a bit."

"I'll still have a job to do," he replied.

"Maybe I'll have to help you more than I have been," she replied, still bent over his wound.

"Would you?" His voice was quiet, pitched for her ears alone, and she looked up at him. And she imagined what it would be like to be Thad's hands for a few days, working by his side, taking his direction… It was a warming thought.

"*Yah*, I would," she said softly.

Thad smiled in response, and she bent over his hand again, this time putting on a stronger, waterproof bandage with more adhesive. She straightened.

"There," she said. "Try moving your fingers now."

Thad wiggled his finger and the bandage stayed in place. *"Danke."*

"My pleasure," she said, and she suddenly realized that the kitchen was quiet. She looked up to see Delia, her mother, and the other women watching them with various expressions on their faces ranging from curiosity to a rather annoying knowing look.

"Thad, you're new to our ways," Delia said as she packed up the cookie tin again. "Have you ever attended an Old Order church service before?"

"No," Thad said. "I came as Lydia's guest."

More knowing looks, and Lydia sighed.

"I could get you a proper hat," Violet piped up. "Yours is all wrong."

Thad touched his hat with a look of surprise. "It's quite similar."

"But not the same," Violet replied primly.

Lydia chuckled and Delia exclaimed something about being polite and hospitality.

"It's okay," Thad said. "If you want to fix me up so that I look more appropriate, I don't mind. If it's okay with your *mamm*."

Delia sighed and threw up her hands.

"I don't mind," she said. "I bought a hat that was the wrong size for Ezekiel, so it's brand new. I just hope we aren't offending you, Thad."

"I'm harder than that to offend," he said.

The women all seemed to relax a little, and Lydia felt her own anxiety lower. He was being an awfully good sport. Violet grinned and headed for the stairs, her footsteps thumping up over their heads. She returned a couple of minutes later with a proper Old Order felt hat.

Thad accepted it with a nod of thanks and replaced his own hat with the new one. It fit him perfectly, and suddenly the Beachy Amish veterinarian was looking a whole lot more Old Order.

"It looks good," Violet declared.

"It does," Lydia agreed, and Thad's amused gaze met hers.

"Consider it a gift," Delia said. "I'm glad it's going to good use."

"I'll be back to attending my own church soon enough," Thad said. "I don't want to put you out."

"Maybe you'll visit," Delia said with the most innocent smile that Lydia didn't believe for one moment.

Thad looked over at Lydia again. "Maybe I will."

And her stomach started to flutter. It wasn't exactly fair to suggest something that appealing. Because proper hat or not, Thad was still Beachy Amish. There was a pickup truck at a garage that confirmed it. And if he visited, she'd only get more attached to the man. He was a little too easy to care for. She swallowed. She couldn't let this roomful of women see how flustered she felt.

"Let me show you how the service will work," Lydia said, changing the subject. "When we sit down, we all go inside according to our ages. The oldest go inside first. So we'll have to see where you fit in. You'll make some new friends, no doubt."

Thad stood up and Lydia gave the women a nod as she headed for the door.

No, Lydia was smarter than to get overly attached to this completely inappropriate man. That was why the bishop had chosen her to begin with. She helped. It was what she did, and she wasn't about to prove the bishop wrong in his choice.

Chapter Seven

That wasn't the first time Thad had been nipped by a horse, and it wouldn't be the last. He felt foolish for having gotten his hand close enough to those teeth, mostly. That, and he was badly bruised. Horses' teeth were sharp enough to break skin, but with a glove on, it was the pressure of the bite that did the most painful damage.

Lydia's bandaging was well done, and he half hoped that it would fall off, just so she'd hold his hand again. That feeling of her soft touch while she bandaged him had left him breathless. Silly of him, he knew, but... Lydia was starting to lodge into his thoughts throughout the day and the evenings, and to have her attention so focused on his injury had been unexpectedly wonderful.

During the service, he'd stolen a couple of looks over at her across the aisle, and her gaze had flickered in his direction at the same time. When that happened, her face would go pink, and the women on either side of her would try to smother smiles.

If he could feel butterflies over her bandaging his hand, then he felt a bit better that she was blushing. Thad had been starting to feel like there was a natural spark between them—friendship, maybe? If she weren't Old

Order, he might think she liked him enough to go out with him, but he knew how things worked out here, and he wasn't in the running for Lydia's attention.

Thad couldn't look at her again, since he was seated right between Jacob Knussli and Joel Beiler. Jacob was the owner of the farm where he'd vaccinated calves, and Joel owned the B&B. So he had to keep up appearances. Just a veterinarian, joining them for a service. He'd better not give them anything to gossip about later!

The sermon was lengthy, and the preacher spoke about humility. It was a familiar subject from sermons in his home church, but the Old Order Amish took the subject a little deeper. He talked about how each of them were of immense value to *Gott*, and that no one was worth more than any other person. He spoke about how *Gott* sent his Son to a poor girl with no important connections. He chose Joseph to be Jesus's father, and Joseph wasn't rich or influential in any way. Jesus himself was born in a stable—an image that the Amish understood better than most. *Gott* showed us what He valued—and *Gott* looked at hearts. Every human being had the same worth before *Gott*, and each one was worth dying for. Therefore, they all must treat each other with compassion and hospitality, and no one should receive better treatment because he or she was considered more important.

Thad thought that over as the lengthy sermon stretched on. Was it so terrible if a man achieved great things because of boyhood insecurity? Couldn't good things come from difficult beginnings? Was it so bad to be proud of his achievements?

But there was something very reassuring about that

sameness in an Old Order community. It was similar in his Beachy Amish community, too, but somehow he'd never been able to settle into community life the way he should have. But sitting on the men's side of the service, he couldn't help but wish he blended in here a little bit better. All those pairs of pants made from the same fabric. All those shoes in similar styles, and the suspenders all bought from the same stores in town, and ordered from the same suppliers.

Yes, it was reassuringly the same, and he could see why they insisted upon it in their *Ordnung*. No man above another. No man of higher value than another… It was a beautiful ideal when it played out in real life.

It didn't always work that way, though. Sometimes, no matter how pure the ideals, there was a sensitive, earnest boy who was left out.

Ahead of him, Nathan Lapp sat with his son at his side. Jonathan leaned over to his father and whispered loud enough for Thad to overhear, "*Daet*, I'm worried about Bobli."

Nathan didn't move, but the boy turned forward again, his shoulders slumping, and Thad's heart went out to the kid. Thad sent up a sincere, silent prayer.

Lord, please let that calf recover. Heal her—I'm not sure that there's much else I can do.

After the service, there was a meal. The men ate together again, and the women ate together. He was able to catch a few minutes alone with Lydia, but she was more bashful then, and he could tell that having her entire community watching her have a conversation with him wasn't comfortable for her.

He spent some time chatting with the farmers, listening about their concerns with their animals and giving some advice where he could. One of the boys was overly interested in veterinarian medicine, and he was quickly whisked away by his father. Thad was useful to the community, but they certainly didn't want their boys following in his footsteps!

When the Speichers were ready to head on home, Thad hitched up that devious betrayer of a horse, and Lydia rode with him behind her parents' buggy as they made their way back to the Speichers' place. He knew his way to the B&B from there.

"Did you enjoy our service?" Lydia asked.

"Very much."

"Really?"

"You think I'd fib about that?" he asked with a chuckle.

"I hope not," she said, no laughter in her tone. Even the thought of an untruth did not amuse her, it seemed.

"I did like it," he said, softening his tone. "I…I felt convicted by the sermon, truthfully."

"Oh… Really? Which part?" Then her face colored and she stammered, "I shouldn't ask that. I'm sorry."

"It's okay," he replied. "It was the part about humility. I was remembering why I studied so hard in school. I was just so lonesome, and if I put my time and energy into grades and degrees, then I didn't have so much time on my hands to face my actual feelings."

"What were you actually feeling?" she asked quietly.

"Lonely, unaccepted, unworthy…" He sighed. "It made me wonder why I still work this hard. Is it because I love my job? Is it because I want to do the best I can with the talents God gave me, or is there still a part of me that hides in the work?"

"Are you still lonely?" she whispered.

He thought about giving the polite answer—a lie—but he couldn't do it. Not with her frank, brown eyes locked on his face like that.

"Yes," he admitted. "Sometimes."

"I was about to say that if you were Old Order you'd never feel lonesome," she said.

"But you won't say it?" he asked.

"I realized it wasn't entirely true. You might have lineups of women trying to get your attention. But I'm devoted to my Old Order faith, and I'm lonely sometimes, too. And I don't have any lineups of suitors."

He reached out and put a hand over hers. He realized belatedly that the gesture wouldn't be welcome, but just as he was about to pull away again, she turned her hand and closed her gloved fingers over his.

His breath caught in his throat. He was holding her hand… Then he saw her touching his wounded finger.

"Does it hurt still?" she asked.

"Not as much," he replied.

She nodded, silent, but still, she didn't let go of his hand, either, and his heart thundered in his own ears. Was she just thinking about his wound, or was this something more? It certainly felt like something more to him.

"I've never been the kind of man who liked lineups of women," he said.

"What?"

"You mentioned lineups of women if I were Old Order," he said. "But I've never needed all sorts of interested women to reassure me that I'm liked. I only ever wanted one woman who'd be everything to me."

Lydia looked up at him, but he had to put his attention back onto the road again because her parents' buggy ahead of them was turning onto their road. He pulled his hand back to rein in Absalom and guide him around the turn onto the gravel road.

When they were around the corner, he allowed himself one quick look in her direction, and he found her gaze locked on him again.

"You'll find her, Thad."

"I hope so," he said, but his voice felt thick. Because right now he found he wasn't longing for some unknown woman out there who'd fill his heart. He'd found the one he wanted—but he couldn't have her.

"I know that we Old Order are different from you Beachy Amish," Lydia said, "but we women can't be so very different. We all want the same thing at heart. So I'll let you in on the secret. That's exactly what every woman wants to hear."

"Is it?" he asked with a short laugh.

"*Yah*. It is." She didn't laugh along with him. She was utterly serious.

The Speicher buggy disappeared into their drive, and Absalom followed, bringing them around that last turn.

"Well, I can tell you one thing men like, Lydia," he said. "And those donuts were really delicious. You said they're something special you'll make for your family— never for sale."

"It's true," she said.

"That's something a man likes to hear," he said, "that

there's something special at home that no one else can enjoy. That's...very sweet."

"Well, we have more donuts inside if you'd like to join us this evening," Lydia said. "*Mamm* made a big batch last time."

The thought of those sweet, fluffy, melt-in-his-mouth confections made his stomach growl.

"I'd love some," he said.

But he noticed that these were her mother's donuts. He had to wonder what Lydia's donuts were like...and if she'd ever permit him to try one.

The truth was, he might never get the chance—and he might never deserve it, either. He wasn't sticking around, and he shouldn't be longing for something reserved for the man who did.

The afternoon passed quickly and bled into evening. They ate donuts, drank coffee, chatted around the table, and then Thad helped Art with the outdoor chores. The older man was strong and steady, and Thad was glad to be able to pitch in and make the chores go a little faster. They cleaned out stalls and refilled water buckets.

And when they were headed back toward the house, Thad's cell phone rang in his pocket. He noticed the call was from the car garage.

"I'd better take this call," Thad said.

"I'm not stopping you," Art replied brusquely.

Thad picked up the call and walked a few paces away from the house.

"Hi, Dr. Miller?" a woman's voice said.

"Yes," he said.

"I'm just calling about your Ford F-150. It's all fixed

and will be ready for you to pick up first thing in the morning. We open at eight."

"Danke," he said, and then winced at the Pennsylvania Dutch word that had slipped out. "I mean…thank you. I'll be there."

"Sure thing," she said cheerily, and hung up.

He noticed then that he'd missed a call earlier and he had a text message waiting. It was from an old college friend named Ethan Smythe who was now a veterinarian for the Pennsylvania Commercial Dairy Association, which was a lucrative group of commercial dairies.

Call me back. We need some help with a case, and I thought of you.

Thad dialed the number and when Ethan picked up, he sounded happy to hear from him.

"It's been a while," Ethan said. "But look, we've got some calves that are all ill with a virus that's spreading through the herd. We've done all the cultures and tests, but this is slightly different from anything else we've dealt with."

Ethan outlined the symptoms, the tests they'd done, the results, and the speed of the spread.

"That's familiar, actually," Thad said. "I've got a client here in Redemption with a calf that is exhibiting the same symptoms. I did the tests, and it looks like it's a virus. I've given the calf some antibiotics in case there is a secondary infection, but that's about all I can do besides tell the owners to keep it warm, give it milk, and… this may very well be the same thing."

"Could be," his friend agreed. "Do you have time to

come out and take a look? Maybe we can find a solution together that'll help us and your client."

"Yes, absolutely," Thad replied. "I can free up most of the day. I can be there by noon."

"But look, Thad. I reached out to you for a reason. We're going to be hiring soon, and I put your name in and said I thought you'd be a good addition to our veterinarian team."

"I've just started a position here with a local veterinarian," Thad said. "I'd hate to leave him in the lurch."

"I get it," his friend agreed. "You're a good guy, but our team leads the veterinarian care for eight commercial dairies. The pay is very good, and this is the kind of step up you don't come across every day."

"How often do they hire there?" he asked.

"This is the first opening in five years."

Thad let out a low whistle. It was a very good opportunity, and it wouldn't come again for a long time.

"So when you come by tomorrow…make nice," Ethan said with a chuckle.

"I'm always nice," Thad laughed.

"You know what I mean. Make a good impression. I'd rather work with a friend than someone else, and I think once you see this place, you'll be sold."

"I appreciate it," Thad said. "I really do. I'll be there by noon."

When he hung up the phone, he looked up to see Lydia on the step watching him. He could feel a gulf widening between them, and he wasn't ready for that yet. They were alone outside for the moment, and he knew he couldn't count on that for long.

"Lydia, my truck is ready, and I've got an appointment about an hour from here tomorrow," he said.

Patricia Johns   115

She came down the steps and tugged her shawl closer around herself. "Okay. So you won't need me?"

"Uh—" He had no right to ask her to come. He knew that. "I didn't say that. Do you want to come along? I mean, if you have something else you need to do, I don't need the help navigating, but I'd like your company, all the same."

The last words came out in a rush, and he held his breath, waiting for her response. Lydia's face brightened and she looked over her shoulder.

"I'd like to come."

"Do you need to ask your *daet*?" he asked.

She gave him a wry little smile. "Thad, I might not be married, but I'm a grown woman. Maybe we can stop by a Costco on the way back and I can get some of my family's groceries. That will make it worthwhile for my parents, too."

"Deal," he said. That was easy enough. "I want to show you a really big dairy."

"Oh. A big farm?" she asked.

He nodded.

"That sounds fun!"

And Thad also wanted to show her the life that was tugging at him. She'd never leave the Old Order—he knew it—but maybe she could help him sort all of this out in his own head. Because two different lifestyles were tugging at him, and Lydia had a way of making everything make sense.

So maybe he did need her help navigating, after all.

Lydia sat with her knees pressed tightly together as they sailed on down the highway. The truck seemed to be running fine, which was a big relief to her. Having damaged his vehicle had been weighing hard on her conscience, but all seemed well now. Thad drove with one hand draped over the steering wheel, his bandaged hand resting on his thigh. He pushed his regular black cowboy hat off his forehead, and somehow it made his blue eyes sparkle with a little more good humor than usual. Or maybe he was just enjoying himself more than usual. He relaxed in a different way in his truck. Thad was quieter and more subdued in a buggy or a sleigh. In the truck, he seemed bigger somehow, stronger, and she found herself feeling swept up in his cheeriness.

"When was the last time you got away from home?" Thad asked.

"When I last went to Costco," she replied with a short laugh. "We hire a driver who takes us there once every few months. It's a really big trip and we load up the back of the van and bring it all back."

"You've got your list?" he asked.

"Oh, *yah*. *Mamm* was thrilled I was able to go without hiring someone. It's not often we can get there without the added expense." She winced. "Oh, Thad, I'm sorry. I'm sounding so cheap and thankless."

"No, you aren't," he replied. "You're being honest. I'd rather hear how you really feel, not some polite chitchat."

Thad shot her a smile, and she found herself smiling back.

"Oh… Well, I'm grateful to get out with you today. This is fun. I don't get to travel outside our community too often, so this is a treat."

He was a treat, she realized in a rush. It wasn't just the chance to see someplace new, or to go to Costco, it was a chance to do it all with Thad. Thad made it more enjoyable, a little lighter and more fun.

"After we visit the dairy, I thought I could take you out for something to eat," he said.

"That sounds nice," she said. "Do you like the hot dogs at Costco?"

"Are you saying that given all the options available to us out here, you want a Costco hot dog?" he asked.

Lydia blinked. "Um…yes?"

"Is that a question, or a fact?" he asked. "Because I'm wanting to take you out, get you something you'll enjoy."

Lydia knew what he meant—that they could go to any restaurant they pleased. They didn't have to worry about distance or buggy parking, but the meals she loved most were in a rather humble location across from the Costco checkout stations, and that could not be helped.

"Well… I really like Costco hot dogs, and on a special day, I like a Costco slice of pizza." If he was going to be generous.

Thad started to laugh, but he shot her a tender look. "If it's what you want, it's what you'll get. A hot dog and a slice of pizza. On me."

Now that was something to look forward to.

There were large signs on the highway announcing the Pennsylvania Commercial Dairy headquarters. It seemed strange to see signs on the highway for a farm. Farms for the Amish consisted of small family operations that were tucked away in the countryside and incredibly difficult to find for UPS delivery people or any visitor at all who didn't grow up in those parts.

Thad signaled a turn and took an exit off the main highway, and they headed down a two-lane road. A cattle transport truck came lumbering toward them and sped past, but she noticed how clean and new the vehicle was. The cattle trailer shone in the sunlight, and she could make out cattle inside.

Ahead there was a large three-story building that looked simple enough—gray metal siding, a big sign that read Pennsylvania Commercial Dairy Association, and lots of windows. It appeared to be an office building with a large parking tarmac out front with at least twenty trucks and cars parked in the spaces. The parking lot had been plowed off, and there was no buggy parking that she could see out here. This was a commercial dairy, not connected to the Amish family-run operations she knew so well.

Beyond that, she could see the sheen of large, low, metal-roofed barns—four that she could make out—the twisting roads connecting them, and beyond were snow-covered fields as far as the eye could see, spotted with cattle that stayed close to large feeders. Several men were visible doing various jobs. One door kept opening up and a spray of hose water came out. Another man was talking to a truck driver next to a large tanker as they hooked up a thick, black hose. It was a busy dairy, and for a moment, she just stared.

"It's really something, isn't it?" Thad said.

"*Yah.* It sure is."

This was a completely different world, the only familiar part of it being the scent of cattle on the air that couldn't be avoided when it came to farming. But other than that, this farm looked like a shiny, immaculate machine—like his pickup truck compared to a buggy. Bigger, stronger, fancier, in every meaning of the words.

Thad pulled into a parking space, and then pulled out his cell phone and typed in a text. Lydia sat there with her hands in her lap, wishing she had her crochet bag with her. Somehow, busying her hands with a familiar project helped to push away the uncertainty and anxiety of a new situation. But she hadn't brought it with her today.

"Are you okay?" Thad asked.

"I'm fine," she said.

"You look nervous," he said. "You're not the one who should be nervous, you know."

"What do you mean?" she asked.

"There is a job opening here," he said.

"Don't you have a job?" she asked, squinting up at him.

"I do, but this would be a big step up for me. It would be a stable position with a lot of upward momentum."

She blinked at him.

"I could make a lot more money," he said. He said that meaningfully, as if it explained everything.

"Oh." She nodded. "And you need more?"

"Well, it would let me get a place with a bit more land. Maybe you can appreciate that. I could have some space, maybe a horse, a dog, a garden."

"I can definitely appreciate that." She leaned forward and looked toward the building. The front door opened and a man in tan pants and a ski jacket came outside. "So do you want to work here?"

"*Yah*, Lydia, I do." He followed her gaze, then waved at the man who was coming in their direction. "That's my friend Ethan. You ready?"

"Of course," she said. They were here for Thad to

explore a job opportunity—that was news. There was nothing wrong with that, but her heart sank in disappointment all the same. He'd said he'd be working in their community, but this place was a whole world away.

"I appreciate you being here." Thad reached over and gave her hand a squeeze. "I don't know why, but I feel like you keep my feet on the ground."

That was a compliment to be sure, but something about this place felt wrong to her. Was it that it was just so fancy, or was there something else nagging at the back of her mind?

Thad got out of the truck first, and then Lydia followed. She slammed the door shut behind her. The men shook hands, and when Thad introduced her, Ethan held out his hand to shake hers, too. Lydia kept her hands clasped in front of her and she shot Thad a panicked look.

"Amish women don't shake hands with men," Thad said.

"Right, I'm sorry," Ethan said. "I didn't realize. So you must be—" Ethan's gaze flicked between them, and before either Thad or Lydia could clarify, he seemed to come to his own conclusion. "It's only right that you come see the setup, too, of course. Pleasure to meet you, Lydia."

Ethan was assuming that she and Thad were romantically connected, she could tell, but correcting him now didn't seem like it would help Thad's chances any, especially since Ethan was now talking to Thad about the setup of the organization and the conversation had moved on.

Ethan took them in his truck down a paved road, past some large milking barns. Cows were plodding patiently inside for noon milking. Past those barns were another set of barns she hadn't seen from the parking lot, and then the road turned and took them down a little hill and toward another two-story building much like the one out front. But this one didn't have the tinted glass in the windows, and it had a corral attached, and what looked like some long, low stables, too. A sign on the side of that building read Veterinarian Services.

"This is where we need your help, Thad," Ethan said. "You were the best in our class when it came to epidemiology. And this respiratory illness is a doozy. I'm grateful you came."

Thad was that good at his job, it appeared, and she looked up at the man with a new respect welling up inside of her. They weren't just here for a job opportunity. They were here because this team of veterinarians needed him.

And as easily as that, Thad could be lured away to bigger, more exciting things. He wasn't Old Order. He wasn't *hers*. It shouldn't matter, but somehow it did. And the worst part was, she understood. How could anyone resist being needed?

Chapter Eight

The Veterinarian Services building gave Thad a little rush of excitement just to look at. There'd be lab space here and treatment rooms that could be sanitized after each bovine patient. This was the kind of state-of-the-art equipment a vet dreamed of working with. So much more precise than working out in a field or in someone else's barn.

But large animal veterinarian work was normally done in fields and on barn floors. That was the nature of the job, unless they transported an animal into the clinic for surgery. Here the medical professionals seemed to have so much at their fingertips.

Ethan gave Thad and Lydia a quick tour of the building. This wasn't a public space, so most of it was empty until needed. Thad stood in the doorway of one of the operating rooms and glanced at Lydia. Her eyes darted around the room, and her lips stayed pressed tightly together.

"Impressed?" he asked.

"Are you?" She looked up at him then, her frank gaze meeting his. Yeah, he could feel his feet hitting the ground again.

"It's an impressive setup." He wanted to explain this to her, make her understand.

Lydia just nodded, and he couldn't tell if she was impressed by all this or not. Maybe she was just overwhelmed, but he was glad to have her with him all the same.

Ethan held a door open for them, then strode briskly down the walkway in front of the stalls that housed sick calves. Each stall was a little room of its own with walls all the way to the ceiling. That would help with containing illness—a luxury most farmers didn't have. In front of each stall there was a hand disinfectant dispenser, and when Thad looked into the stalls as they passed, each space was clean and softly lit for the sick animal's comfort.

Thad's stride was longer than Lydia's and he could feel her panting as she tried to keep up. Instinctively, Thad stretched his hand back, and he almost apologized, but then she caught his hand and he tugged her in next to his side, and he smiled to himself.

Somehow, it felt right to have her this close, but his heartbeat was galloping as he realized the importance of holding her hand. From the woman who wouldn't shake hands with a man, this was…special.

Except it wasn't exactly unheard of. It was perfectly normal for people who were courting. Was that the message he wanted to give her? The problem was, he found himself reluctant to let go of her warm fingers, even with all those uncertainties swimming through his mind.

When they got to an end stall, Ethan stopped and Thad released Lydia's hand and leaned against the rail.

A bull calf lay in a bed of clean straw, and his eyes looked sunken.

"May I?" Thad asked, and Ethan gave him a curt nod.

He opened the door and went inside. The animal had a mark and a small shaved spot on his neck—he'd had an IV recently, by the looks of it, and it had bled a little bit. He stroked the calf's ears and they felt cold to the touch. His hand ached where the horse had bitten him, but he pushed that aside, his mind on the animal in front of him. The calf's nose—which would normally be wet in a healthy calf—was dry. This calf looked a whole lot like Bobli did.

Gott, give me wisdom, he silently prayed. *Not just for this calf, but for Bobli, too.*

"This animal is dehydrated," Thad said, looking back at Ethan.

"We've been trying some different medications, but nothing is working," Ethan said.

"This calf won't make it," Thad said frankly. And then an idea came to his mind. There were two medications that didn't combine well, but worked well separately. If only they could function together...

"I have an idea," Thad said. "It's risky, but it might be this calf's last hope."

He explained his theory. They were battling a virus that taxed the animal's immune system to such an extent that most of the young animals died. But if they could allow that immune system to rest a little bit and get some help from some very strong medications, it just might be enough... Not a long-term medication regimen, just one quick blast.

"Those meds are contraindicated," Ethan said.

"I know. And it might mean this animal dies all the same, but if we don't do anything this one won't make it to tomorrow."

Ethan nodded. "That's why you're here. Do what you need to do, and let's see if together we can get this under control."

For the next few minutes, Thad got busy getting another IV ready for the calf. He retrieved a bag of saline and the two medications that he thought just might work this time. When he came back to the stall, he found Lydia squatted next to the calf, a hand on his thin neck. She looked like an old-fashioned army nurse hunkered down there with her white *kapp* covering her hair and the white apron over her blue dress. She was an oddly reassuring sight, like one of the nightingales.

"Poor thing," Lydia murmured.

"I wonder if you could give me a hand," Thad said, and he hung the saline bag on a hook on the wall especially for that purpose. He handed her a packaged sterilized IV needle and squatted down next to her. "Could you open that for me?"

Lydia tore it open and Thad pulled the needle out of the package.

The calf was too weak to offer any resistance, and he felt for the calf's jugular vein.

"Will this work?" Lydia asked.

"I truly hope so," he replied.

"Can you use one of those disinfectant pads to clean this area?" He circled it with his finger.

Lydia tore one open and did a good job of wiping off the already shaved spot on the calf's neck. He worked quickly to insert the IV catheter into the vein and taped it down. Then he attached the tube from the IV bag and started the saline drip. He used a syringe to add the first medication slowly into the line.

"You're okay, little one," Lydia said quietly.

After he'd added the next medication, he covered the calf with a warming blanket, and he offered Lydia a hand to help her stand up. She accepted his aid and he tugged her to her feet.

"A few days ago you wouldn't shake my hand," he said, catching her gaze.

Her face flushed, then she shrugged. "A few days ago, you were a stranger."

Thad knew it was more than that—at least he felt like there was more on his side. He leaned against the railing and she settled next to him as they turned their attention toward the calf.

"Are you really considering coming to work here?" Lydia asked quietly.

"I haven't been offered the job yet," he replied.

"If they offered, though..."

Thad didn't like to consider things too seriously before he knew what was being offered, but when he looked over at her again, he found her worried gaze fixed on the calf.

"What do you think about this place?" he asked.

"It's very fancy."

He could understand her perspective, there. She was used to an Amish farm, and this place had all the bells and whistles. He was thinking of more than just the job, though. Somehow, everything here had become entangled with thoughts of Lydia, and suddenly in a few days he'd gone from a young vet looking to grow in his career to a man who couldn't quite imagine not ever seeing this woman again.

"It's pretty close to your home, though," he said. "I could...visit."

Lydia shot him a look from the corner of her eye.

"What? You don't want me to visit?" he asked with a low laugh.

"I do want you to visit," she said, and she swallowed hard. "But you'd be visiting in a pickup truck, with your fancy cowboy hat, and your fancy plaid shirts, and your pants that are all kinds of wrong."

"My pants are that wrong?" Thad looked down at his jeans. "Denim is durable."

"So are our broadfall pants."

"I'm not Old Order," he said.

She smiled faintly. "Exactly."

Did that mean they couldn't be friends? He pushed the thought back. She was here with him, wasn't she? And today wasn't about her helping him navigate. She was here because she wanted to be.

The calf stirred, and Thad pushed himself off the rail and hunkered down next to the small animal. He ran a hand over the calf and pulled open one eyelid to look at the eye. It looked clearer. Thad checked the animal's temperature, and the fever had reduced by a whole degree. That was a very good sign.

They sat there together as the minutes ticked by. Twenty minutes. Thirty. Forty. He liked having Lydia here with him. She was comforting to more than the sick animal.

Thad stroked a hand over the calf's ears, and they felt warmer, too. The calf was no longer seeming so dehydrated thanks to the saline drip, but it was more than that.

"I think the medication combo is working," he said.

"Is it?" Lydia came to his side and squatted down next to him, her earlier reservations apparently forgotten. She reached out and ran a hand down the calf's muzzle.

"If the medication was going to cause problems combined the way it is, we'd see it by now," Thad said. "And this is definitely a positive direction."

"Have you found the solution to this illness?" Lydia asked.

"Maybe." He rose to his feet, but somehow he felt that it was more than a maybe. "Lydia, I think we've just saved a whole generation of calves at this farm."

"And Bobli?" she asked.

"I think so."

Lydia's eyes lit up and she broke into the most stunning smile he'd ever seen. His breath caught in his throat and he felt almost lightheaded looking down at her. He should get some space—this wasn't quite safe with eyes as bright as hers and a heart as wayward as his was right now... He put a hand on her waist to steady himself to slip past, but she moved at the same time he did, and she collided with his chest, a soft puff of air touching his lips.

"Oh!" she gasped.

"Sorry, I—" But Lydia was right there. So close, and he had tried to get some space from her for this very reason. Because now that he was standing there with a hand on her soft waist and her lips so close to his, he couldn't force himself to move again.

"You did it, Thad," she whispered.

He had—with God's help, and hers, too. And while

he was glad he'd be able to alleviate the suffering, he found himself thinking more about her lips than anything else. And then, before he could think better of it, he dipped his head down just a whisper from her lips, and he paused there, waiting for her to step back.

"Lydia," he whispered. He wasn't sure if he meant it as a warning, or if he just wanted to say her name, but then he felt her lips brush his ever so lightly, and he lowered his lips the rest of the way to cover hers.

She sank into his arms, and he felt a flood of relief wash over him. This was what he didn't know he'd been wanting all this time, but now that he had her in his arms, it felt right. So very, very right.

She pulled back slightly, and he broke off the kiss. Her eyes fluttered open and she stared at him, wide-eyed.

"That was a kiss," she breathed.

"Yeah, that was," he agreed. That had been the first kiss of his life that had included his entire aching heart, and he was both overwhelmed and suddenly a little afraid of what it meant.

"I've never done that before," she said.

His heart pounded to a stop. He was her first kiss! As if this couldn't get more complicated, because something had broken open inside of him when he'd kissed her, and he wasn't sure he could put it all back together again.

Footsteps sounded down the hallway and Lydia quickly stepped back just as Ethan appeared at the stall doorway.

"How's it going?" Ethan asked, and for a moment a shadow passed over his gaze as if he realized he'd interrupted something.

"Thad did it," Lydia announced, her voice jubilant. "The calf is improving. The medication worked!"

And Thad felt his heart soar. Yes, he'd found a solution with God's help, but the warm pride in her voice would do more for him than any accolades from his peers. She was impressed, and he wished he could kiss her all over again.

The farmland whisked past the passenger-side window of Thad's pickup truck, and Lydia sucked in a wavering breath. They had stayed another couple of hours before Thad packed up some of the medication for Bobli and they'd headed back toward home... But those last two hours had consisted of a strange magnetic draw between them. When they walked, they found their fingers brushing. When they observed a calf, Thad's pant leg would brush against her dress. And more than once he'd offered her his hand to help her stand back up again after she'd been crouched down for a few minutes and her knees were getting sore from the position.

And she'd liked it. She'd more than liked that connection between them. This was the first time she'd had this kind of mutual attraction with any man! Men just didn't seem to see her that way, but Thad did. Thad seemed to recognize the woman in her, and her stomach was still fluttering in response.

And she'd kissed him. The realization of what she'd done was only now sinking in as they headed down the highway toward Redemption. There was a strange freedom that came with that commercial dairy. No expectations. No judgment.

"You okay?" Thad asked.

She cast him a shaky smile. "I'm realizing that I kissed you."

"Well, in all fairness, there were both of us involved in that," he said, but she saw some color hit his cheeks. It was gratifying to know he was capable of embarrassment, too.

"We don't do that," she said. "I mean, we Old Order women. We don't kiss men. We don't…date casually. We date with the intent to marry, and if there isn't hope of marriage in that relationship, we don't let it go further."

Thad was silent, and Lydia licked her lips. Maybe it was different for them, and maybe he needed to understand this.

"It's only proper," she went on. "It…it protects us from being used."

"You think I'm using you?" Thad glanced over at her, his warm brown eyes filled with concern. "Because I'm not. I'd never do that. We Beachy Amish don't play around with these kinds of feelings, either, you know. I mean, we do date. We get to know someone, and we try to find someone we can marry." His grip on the steering wheel was white-knuckled. "But I'm not just playing around here, Lydia."

"I'm sorry. I didn't mean to imply—" But she actually had meant what she said. "Thad, we have no future."

"I know." His voice was low and quiet, almost covered over by the rumble of the truck's engine.

"And I know that, too," she said. "I have just as much responsibility here. Maybe even more, because I am Amish enough to know better, as my father would put it." It felt good to be able to talk about this plainly. It felt like the knots inside of her were starting to loosen.

"You know, sometimes...things happen," he said quietly.

"What does that mean?" she asked, turning toward him in the seat and giving the seat belt a tug to give her some room to move. "Things happen? Of course they do, but we have choices!"

He reached out and took her hand, his grip firm, warm and reassuring.

"Hey," he said. "That was your first kiss."

"Yah." She wished she sounded stronger, more confident.

"Well, sometimes when a man and a woman feel a powerful connection, they tumble past the lines of strict friendship. They might walk more closely together, or start holding hands without even thinking about it."

Like now? But his hand over hers felt intentional, and it was oddly comforting. He gave her hand a little squeeze as if acknowledging the irony there.

"What I'm trying to say," Thad went on, "is that our kiss wasn't planned. We didn't think it through, or weigh the real likelihood of us having a future together. We just...felt something very strongly, and we shared a moment."

"I don't like that." She pulled her hand free of his. It was too easy to hold his hand, too easy to feel like she could lean into his strength. "I don't play with moments. I'm worth a lifetime."

"I'm sorry," Thad said. "I know you are. You're wonderful, but I shouldn't have kissed you."

"I'm not blaming you!" she said earnestly. "I...started it."

And Lydia knew it was true. For the first time in her

life she'd been so close to a man who just seemed to melt when he looked at her—a good man. A strong, capable, moral man. And she'd closed that distance between them.

"Lydia, why don't we just agree that we won't do it again?" he said.

Lydia stilled. The kiss had happened. There was no taking it back, but maybe he was right. They were both strong, moral people. If they'd thought it through now and knew there was no future between them, could they simply stop this?

"We can do that?" she asked.

"I can."

She looked over at him in startled surprise. "Oh!"

Thad shot her a rueful grin. "I'll tell you what. I solemnly promise you, Lydia, that I will not kiss you again unless you ask me to."

"What?" She felt the heat hit her face.

"It's not right to promise you can't deliver," Thad said. "And if you asked me to kiss you, I couldn't say no. I'd certainly kiss you. So that's why I'm including that—just for honesty's sake. But unless that very unlikely circumstance arises, I promise to not kiss you again."

Was that enough? It did make her feel a little more stable, a little less at the mercy of these wild and growing feelings between them.

"Okay," she said. "We simply won't kiss each other again."

"Because we're mature, competent adults," Thad said.

"We are," she agreed. "It's a deal, Thad."

He smiled again, and she leaned back in the seat feeling better. They just wouldn't do it. That should take care of things, shouldn't it?

"Now," Thad said. "Let's find Costco."

The wholesale club store was busy that afternoon, and Lydia followed her list closely. They needed oatmeal, honey, dried fruit and some large bottles of cinnamon, nutmeg and cloves. Thad pushed the cart, and Lydia led the way round the store. There were several Amish families shopping there—there was always a few in this Costco—and while Lydia would normally say hello to them, even if she didn't know them personally, this time she did her best to avoid anyone who looked Amish in the least. She wasn't sure why… Maybe she just didn't want to have to explain Thad to anyone when she could hardly explain him to herself.

One family consisted of a portly older woman with several teenagers along with her. They were piling their cart high with grocery staples, and in order to avoid them, Lydia whisked down an aisle, and it was only when she was halfway down it with Thad behind her with the cart that she realized it was the Christmas decoration aisle.

There were Christmas tree balls, outdoor lights, Santa Claus decorations and miniature villages all lit up and playing little tunes. There were nutcrackers in their red-and-gold suits in various sizes—one that stood almost five feet tall! Some items only had a few left, this being just days before Christmas Eve, and at the far end of the aisle there was a massive inflatable snowman on display that would go in some Englisher's yard.

The ornaments were pretty—she had to admit that—

but there was something empty about all the displays that she couldn't quite put her finger on. The only word that came to her mind was *fancy*, but it was more than that.

"Do you use these things?" Lydia asked, turning back to Thad.

Thad leaned his elbows onto the cart handle, his dark brown gaze following her patiently. He flicked his hat higher on his forehead.

"No. My parents have a little stable and manger, and we decorate with holly and evergreen boughs."

Lydia scanned the aisle once more, her gaze landing on an ornament that showed little children looking up at a jolly Santa Claus with joy on their faces. She wondered why it gave her such an uncomfortable feeling. What did it matter? It was just a little holiday fun played by people who didn't live a plain life.

"Let's go pay," Thad suggested, his deep voice pulling her out of her thoughts. "You must be hungry."

She was, and they went through the checkout line. She paid with the cash her mother had given her, and then they went to the food counter to order the hot dogs and slices of pizza.

A few minutes later, eating the delicious food and feeling her mood start to settle now that her stomach was filling, Lydia wiped her mouth with a napkin.

"I know what bothers me about those Christmas decorations," she said.

"What's that?" Thad asked. He took a jaw-cracking bite of pizza. He'd been hungry, too, it seemed.

"I see it all—the glitter and lights and bright colors— and what is it all about?" she asked. "It's about presents. Gifts. Shiny paper. But what about after Christmas?"

She took another bite of her hot dog, chewing thoughtfully.

"It all goes into storage, I suppose," Thad replied.

"I suppose," she agreed. "But Christmas is supposed to last. And what do we long for most this time of year? Comfort in the face of hard times. Reassurance that we aren't alone and that no matter what comes our way, there is a bigger plan at work. We want family. Connections. Relationships."

Romance—the lasting kind. But she didn't want to say that out loud.

"The older we get, the deeper our needs," he murmured.

"That sums it up rather well," she said. "The older I get, the deeper my needs, too."

Lydia needed more than what she had—her brother wasn't wrong about that. But maybe it wouldn't come from a marriage and home of her own. Maybe *Gott* would guide her on a different adventure. Who knew?

But she knew with unwavering certainty that she needed more, and if Jesus's birth that went against all expectations was any kind of predictor, *Gott* would provide for her in an unexpected way.

She just had to trust her Maker.

Chapter Nine

They arrived at Nathan Lapp's farm late in the afternoon. The sun was still shining warm and bright over a trampled front yard. A teenager was sweeping off the front porch, and Nathan's wife, Katie, stood on the side porch, pulling on a squeaking clothesline. She was taking frost-covered clothes down, hitting them against the rail to knock off the snow and frost, and laying them one on top of another in a stack of frozen clothing. She'd hang them on clothes racks to dry the rest of the way inside.

This was the kind of life that Lydia longed for—marriage, *kinner*, a whole family's load of laundry to do each week. She longed for wedding vows, and decades spent with one man as they built a life together. And she wanted it so badly these days that sometimes it hurt.

Katie gave Lydia a friendly wave. They often sat together during quilting nights when the women would get together and make large, intricate quilts to be sold off at the community mud sales when they made money for projects like sprucing up the school house, or building up their emergency medical fund. And Katie was a friendly, animated woman to sit with, although she was a few years older than Lydia. She was full of husband-hunting advice, too, although it hadn't been much help to Lydia yet.

"Hello!" Katie called.

"Hello, Katie," Lydia said. "How is Bobli doing?"

"The calf?" Katie rubbed her cold, reddened hands together. "Jonathan has been with her all day. I had to send his brother with his lunch because Jonathan wouldn't leave his calf's side. But she's holding on."

"We have a possible cure," Thad said. "But I need to talk to your husband about it. It's isn't cheap, but…it's worked on some other calves."

"Nathan is in the barn this time of day," Katie said, and she pointed in the direction of a red barn beyond. "Do you need me to walk with you out there?"

"No, no," Thad said. "We can find our way. Thank you."

The clothesline squeaked as Katie pulled on it again, and Lydia and Thad headed off through the gate and toward the big barn. The sound of cardboard-hard clothing being whacked against the railing echoed behind them, and Lydia made a point of walking a proper eighteen inches away from Thad. They were no longer on a commercial dairy. This was Amish property, and Lydia had a reputation to watch.

Thad pushed open the barn door and stepped back to let her go inside first. It was a polite gesture, and as she passed him to go inside, her shoulder brushed his chest, and she found herself overwhelmed with the temptation to linger there. She wouldn't, though. The barn was dim, and there was a kerosene lamp lit on the far side. There was the scrape of a stool against the cement floor and Nathan stood up.

"Oh, Thad. Did I forget an appointment?" Nathan asked.

"I came by to see the calf," Thad said, and as he slipped past Lydia, his hand touched the small of her back. Then he was gone as he headed over to the stall where the little calf lay. Lydia exhaled a shaky breath.

When she got to the stall, Thad had put his bag down on the straw next to him and he was pulling back the calf's eyelids and he pulled out a stethoscope to listen to the heartbeat. Jonathan sat in the straw next to his calf, looking somber. His parents had probably already prepared him for the possibility that this calf wouldn't make it. That was farm life.

"I have a possible cure," Thad said, sitting back on his heels and looking up at Nathan. "But it isn't cheap."

Nathan sighed and pulled his hat off his head. He rubbed a hand through his sparse hair, then replaced the hat.

"What kind of cure?"

"Two medications that normally don't work well together, but have been making a very big difference for some calves with the same illness at another farm," Thad said, pushing himself back to his feet.

"Expensive, though?" Nathan asked.

The men moved off a few paces, and Lydia watched them go. They'd talk cost now, and Nathan would have a choice to make.

"I have some money of my own saved," Jonathan said, looking at Lydia pleadingly. "I'd give my own money for the medicine for Bobli."

Lydia squatted down next to the boy, and she pet the calf's shoulder gently.

"All of Bobli's life you've loved her," Lydia said. "Bobli has known deep, solid love all this time. That's something very special."

"I want Bobli to get better!" A tear leaked down the boy's cheek.

"We'll do our best," Lydia assured him. "But you know how it is. Life and death are in *Gott*'s hands, not ours."

"I've prayed," the boy said earnestly.

"Me, too, Jonathan," she said. "I'm praying for Bobli, too."

The men came back over then, and Lydia noticed a change in Thad. He looked more somber, a little angry, even. But he pulled out his supplies to set up an IV for the calf. Lydia recognized the process now.

"Now, Bobli is a very sick calf," Thad said to Jonathan. "I'm going to give her some medicine that has helped other calves, and I hope it will help her, too. But I can't promise. She's very sick."

Jonathan nodded eagerly.

"I'll need you to step out of the stall so I can work," Thad said to the boy.

Jonathan reluctantly got up and stepped out, then Thad got to work. The IV was inserted, the medication was administered, and then Jonathan went back to sit with his calf. She thought she saw Thad's lips move in a silent prayer, then he packed up his supplies.

"*Danke*, Nathan," Thad said, shaking the other man's hand.

Nathan didn't answer, and Thad met Lydia's gaze and then nodded toward the door. They were finished here. They'd done all they could.

Back in the truck, Thad seemed to be driving more slowly heading back to her home.

"What's the matter?" Lydia asked.

"He didn't want to treat the calf," Thad said.

"What? He called you in last time. He's changed his mind?"

"He thought it was too expensive. And when I asked what his son would think if he didn't at least try, he said that his son would get over it." Thad's tone was incredulous. "You saw that boy. You saw how much he loves that calf… What kind of father does that?"

Lydia didn't have an answer for him, because she didn't know.

"But you gave the calf the medication," she said.

"I'm not charging him. I'll pay for it myself," Thad said. "But the veterinarian who passes through should never have more compassion on a boy than the father does. That's just wrong."

"He's strict," Lydia said softly. "But he loves him."

She knew that Nathan and Katie loved all of their *kinner* dearly. Jonathan was a very loved boy.

"It's hard for a family to afford extra expense sometimes," Lydia added, feeling the need to defend this family again.

"It isn't that," Thad said. "Nathan told me that animals dying was just how life went, and sparing Jonathan that pain wasn't helping. You know the dog I lost as a boy? Well, he didn't die. His name was Fluff, and he wasn't well-behaved. My father made me give him up to a family in the country. He said it was better for the dog, but he hadn't understood how much I loved that dog…"

Thad's voice trailed off, and Lydia's heart tugged. "So…you just had to say goodbye?"

"I did."

"Did you get another pet?" she asked.

"No," Thad said. "And there was no replacing him. And there was also no discussion. My father didn't want any more animals in the house. As an adult I understand that some dogs do better with more space. That was the case for Fluff. But some boys need more compassion, too."

"And that was the case for you," she said.

"Yeah, it was."

Once upon a time, he'd been a sensitive boy, too. And somehow that touched her heart. He'd been a boy who loved deeply, and she'd seen a part of the grown man who could care very deeply, too.

Lydia was silent for a moment, and they slowed for the turn onto her road. She might be falling for him, but he was still a man who was in a new community for a short period of time and who needed compassion. Somehow, she needed him to see a different side to their community—the faith-filled, loving, dedicated side.

"Thad, would you like to come to dinner?" she asked.

Thad looked over at her, and for a moment, he looked undecided. "Is that wise?"

"We'll be surrounded by my family," she said with a joking little smile. "You can't possibly kiss me."

Thad laughed and shook his head. "I said you'd have to ask me, and I mean that."

"Is that a yes to dinner?" she asked.

"That's a yes to dinner."

* * *

Thad sat at the kitchen table with Art Speicher, the women bustling in the kitchen. The aroma of sizzling sausages and brown-buttered noodles filled the kitchen, making his stomach rumble in anticipation of the meal. There were some cut vegetables in a pot on the big, black wood stove, and if Willa and Lydia cooked like the women in his family, the vegetables starting to boil was the cue that everything would be ready soon. Somehow, he didn't doubt that Willa and Lydia would be just as perfectly timed as his own mother was.

Thad's gaze moved toward Lydia—tall, slim, graceful. He couldn't help but remember that kiss they'd shared in the stable, and he wondered what would happen to their easy friendship now. He was glad she'd asked him for dinner because it meant that she wasn't pulling away, but...maybe she should. Maybe *he* should, for that matter. He was feeling more for Lydia than was good for him, and he knew it. But he'd never come across a woman quite like her before, either. She was a strange mix of solemnity and suddenly bubbling laughter, and he couldn't help but wonder if he'd be able to see more of her after Dr. Ted came back, or if that window between their worlds would close.

Would this time together be chalked up to charity on her part? That thought stung, because this time with her had made him feel more alive than he'd ever felt before.

Lydia seemed to sense his eyes on her because she glanced over her shoulder and her cheeks pinked. He'd said he wouldn't kiss her again unless she asked him to, and he meant to stand by that promise. But there was a small, wicked part of him that hoped she'd ask. He cleared his throat and dropped his gaze.

"So, how did you find using the sleigh for a few days?" Art asked, pulling Thad's attention away from Lydia.

Right. He shouldn't be staring at the man's daughter. He tried to push back a surge of embarrassment at having been caught in the act.

"It was a nice experience," Thad said. "You said before that God never intended us to move as fast as we do in our trucks and cars, and I think I see your point. The sleigh gave me time to think."

"Aha!" Art said, waggling his finger at him. "That's the secret. A man needs to think, not react. That right there is the difference between men of character and men of the world. A man needs time to mull things over, to know why he thinks what he does, to understand the layers of his own emotions. And that takes time. Our way of life provides that time."

"We Beachy Amish are certainly a slower pace than the rest of America," Thad said. "We don't have TV to watch, and we don't listen to radio in our vehicles. We do things differently."

"But we Old Order take it at a slower pace, still," Art pointed out. "We move at the pace of a horse's trot. That's fast enough when there are countless things a man needs to think through to be sure of himself."

"I can appreciate that now," Thad said.

"And the care of a horse adds another level to the patience that is developed," Art went on. "A man has a relationship with his horse. He cares for him, and grooms him, and calls in a vet when he needs to. A horse is a long-term investment, and it forces us to live in places that have the space to house a horse. It keeps us with enough land to garden, enough land to let an animal graze. We stay connected to the earth, to our gardens, to our animals and our families."

"My career is spent in supporting the health of horses and cattle, so I spend a lot of time out here in farms and acreages. A rural life is a sweet one."

"Where do you live?" Art asked.

"In town."

"Ah." Art nodded slowly.

"I don't have a horse to care for," Thad said, feeling the need to defend himself, somehow. "But we live simply. We buy items used and fix what breaks. My mother made the curtains in my apartment by hand. She wove the rag rug by my door, too. I made the table and chairs with my father in his workroom."

"You live alone?" Art asked.

"I do. I live in an apartment in Evansburgh. But I still live simply. If I can buy something used, I do. I don't follow fads. I don't throw an item away unless it can't be fixed. I have kitchen pots that have been in the family for longer than any of us remember. I have the strainer that my grandmother used, and a rotary egg-beater that's been in the family for a few generations. I don't live a fancy life."

"And our church service? How did you find it?"

"I'm used to meeting in a church building," he admitted. "But I enjoyed the sermon a lot. It is quite similar to Beachy Amish preaching, honestly."

"Hmm." Art didn't seem to like hearing that.

"Do you really preach the same way about humility?" Willa called from the sink where she was rinsing lettuce.

"Yes, it's quite similar," Thad said. "And I know we aren't quite as separated from the world as you are, but we still dress differently. While I know my hat is far too fancy for an Old Order community, and my clothes are, too, when you put me in the middle of Englisher society, I stand out like a sore thumb."

"But your pace of life—" Art said.

"It's faster than yours," Thad agreed, "but we're still moving much slower than everyone else around us. I didn't appreciate that until I was in university and studying to be a veterinarian. I got a good look at the regular American lifestyle, and we Beachy Amish are considered dinosaurs to everyone else."

"The things that matter take more time to appreciate," Art said firmly.

"I fully agree," Thad replied.

Art met Thad's gaze for a moment, then narrowed his eyes. "Do you know how to play Dutch Blitz?"

"Of course." Thad shot him a grin. Dutch Blitz was the only card game besides Uno that he'd been permitted to play, and he and his siblings used to play it for hours.

"Aha!" Art said, pushing back his chair. "I'll get the game!"

Art disappeared down a hallway, and Thad found Lydia looking at him with a grin on her face.

"My father is very competitive in Dutch Blitz," she said.

"I grew up with five siblings," he chuckled. "I can hold my own. Why don't you come play with us?"

"Go on," Willa said. "Dinner's almost ready. If you play, it'll go faster, and then we can eat."

Lydia took a towel off her shoulder and hung it up,

then came around the counter and slid into a kitchen chair opposite her father's. Her eyes were bright in anticipation of the game, and he wondered just how competitive this family got with a good game of Dutch Blitz.

Art returned with a pack of Dutch Blitz cards wrapped in a rubber band and he slid back into his chair.

"Ah, you're playing, too, Lydia?" he asked.

"For sure and certain," she said.

"Lydia is some real competition with this game," Art said. "All right. Let's play."

Art shuffled the cards, then lined them up in front of each of them according to the rules. There was a line of cards to work from in front of each person, and a stack of cards in each of their hands they could flip through. Thad and his siblings used to play this game at a breakneck speed, and the adults had never been able to keep up with their nimble flipping of cards.

Thad stretched his legs out under the table and he felt his shoes touch Lydia's. He knew it was hers because her gaze flickered toward him. But she didn't move her feet, and he didn't move his, either. It felt nice to be this close to her.

"And...start!" Art called out.

They all started flipping through the cards in their hands as quickly as they could to find the cards that would start the game in earnest. Lydia was fast, too, as she flipped through her cards, and slapped a blue number one card down in the center. Art slapped down an orange number one next to it, and the game was off. Cards hit the table with a thump as they slapped them down and continued their search. Thad shot his hand out with a card to go onto one of the piles, and he put his down a fraction of a second before Art's came, and the older man groaned.

"You're fast, Thad!" Art laughed. "I'll give you that!"

Flip, flip, flip. Thump, thump, thump…

Thad shot his hand out at the same time as Lydia, but he slowed and let her get there first.

"Aha! You're letting her get it!" Art said. "Don't feel sorry for Lydia—" He slapped down another card. "She doesn't need the charity, trust me." He slapped down another one.

Thad felt a little embarrassed to have been caught at it, and when he glanced over at Lydia, her shining gaze met his in a way that made his heart skip a beat.

The piles of cards grew and their own stores of cards dwindled until Thad slapped down his last card and won the game. Lydia was laughing, breathless and cheeks flushed. Art threw up his hands—he'd only had three cards left.

"Good game," Thad said.

"We have to play again!" Art said. "Let me shuffle—"

There was a knock at the side door then, and everyone stopped. Art got up, and Lydia took over corralling all the cards and tapping them back into a single deck again. Art opened the door to find another Amish man standing there. His voice was just loud enough for Thad to make out his Pennsylvania Dutch words.

"I'm collecting for Benjamin Lapp's daughter, Mary Schrock," the man said. "The baby came early, so there's going to be time in the Greenberg Hospital for both mother and child. There's no way around it."

"Ah…" Art's voice turned sad. "Poor girl. Is Mary doing all right?"

"From what I understand, she's still quite ill," he replied. "We'll all need to help them."

"Of course, of course," Art said, and he looked across the kitchen toward his wife, who was drying her hands on a towel, her expression concerned.

"That's Deacon Earl," Lydia murmured softly for Thad's ears alone.

"Is it a boy or a girl, Earl?" Willa asked.

"A baby boy. He's only three pounds," Earl replied. "Benjamin and Anna are at the hospital with their daughter right now. They telephoned their Amish neighbor with the news of the *bobli*'s arrival."

"Willa, let's go to the study and see what we can give," Art said.

Willa nodded and joined her husband.

"May I use your facilities?" Deacon Earl asked delicately.

"*Yah*, of course," Art said with a brisk nod, and as quickly as that, the entire kitchen emptied. Art and Willa headed down the hallway and a door shut with a click behind them, and Earl headed up the stairs for the washroom. The only sound in the kitchen was the soft pinging of the stovepipe.

Thad looked over at Lydia, and she tapped the cards into a neat pile and left them on the tabletop.

"Mary is two years younger than I am," Lydia said, pushing back her chair. "This is her first *bobli*."

Lydia stood up and all of the earlier laughter seemed to have evaporated from the room.

"Is she a good friend?" he asked.

"*Yah*, I've known her since we were tiny." Lydia's gaze met his and he reached out and caught her hand.

She didn't pull back. "She was able to get married. I spent two years being so jealous of her that I had to pray daily for *Gott* to release me from it."

"Getting married seems easier for some," he said.

"Yah." She dropped her gaze.

"I felt some jealousy for other men who are already married with little kids, too," he said. "It's not just women who struggle with that."

Thad stepped a little closer, and she looked up at him, her eyes brimming with an unnamable emotion.

"It's hard to be different," she breathed.

He nodded wordlessly. It was incredibly hard being different—especially when he was looking down at a woman who seemed to be different in the same ways he was, but they came from different worlds. He and Lydia were alike in the ways that mattered to him, but not quite enough to bridge that gap between their cultures.

"I pray that my friend's baby is strong and healthy and *Gott* protects him," Lydia said.

"Amen," he murmured.

"Her husband Leonard is a good man, too," Lydia said. "I'm getting used to watching my friends' milestones from the outside."

Suddenly, he had an image in his mind of Lydia at home in his little apartment in Evansburgh. He could see her cooking with those pots that had lasted generations, and whisking up a meringue with that rotary eggbeater. He could see her in her apron and *kapp*, a smile on her face and flour on her hands, and the thought was so sweet that it brought a lump to his throat.

But he couldn't ask her to leave her family and her

faith behind. Because while it would be perfect for him, he knew it would be far from perfect for her.

The current sadness in her eyes was almost jarring compared to the laughter of moments earlier, and he was suddenly tempted to tip her chin up and kiss her. Maybe he wanted to comfort her…maybe he wanted to comfort himself. But he'd made a promise, and he would keep it.

The sound of footsteps made Thad take a purposeful step back, and he licked his lips, allowing his gaze to meet hers for a just a moment before he dropped it and her parents returned to the room. The stairs creaked, and Earl came back down, too.

Their moment of solitude was over.

Lydia remained silent while her parents passed some bills over to Earl's keeping. Thad took out his wallet and added the cash he had on hand to theirs, as well. It sounded like a young family needed all the help they could get. Hospitalizations were expensive for people who didn't believe in formal insurance.

"*Danke* for helping," Earl said. "Oh—Lydia. My wife asked me to tell you that the van we hired for tomorrow's trip to the hospital to bring those toys for the *kinner* there canceled on us due to illness. I'm sorry."

"It's all right," Lydia said. "There are bigger problems in our community."

Earl said goodbye, then headed back outside to his waiting buggy. Art closed the door after him.

"My, my," Willa tutted. "A little boy born so early…" She heaved a sigh. "May *Gott* be his strength. Lydia, I'm sorry about the canceled van. Maybe we can get a taxi? But those are so very pricey these days…"

"You need to get to the hospital?" Thad asked.

"I was going to the hospital to bring my crocheted toys for the sick children," Lydia said. "I suppose I can go another time. We'll sort something out."

But all Thad could see was another chance to spend time with her, and he couldn't help but jump at it.

"I can drive you out there," Thad said. "If you're willing to go after lunchtime."

"Yah." Lydia brightened. "If you'd drive me, I'd be very grateful."

"I'll come by at one," he said.

Thad stood next to the table, his heart feeling strangely drawn to this little faith community. It wasn't an easy life, though. It was a hard one, and that small community would shoulder all of the burdens together. They dug deep and helped each other.

There was a beauty in that plain life, but there was also hardship, and Thad had to admire the people who chose such obvious difficulty as their norm.

"Let's eat," Willa said with some forced cheeriness, and she put some hot pads on the table. A bowl of brown-buttered noodles followed, a heaping dish of boiled broccoli, and a platter of sausages.

They all took a seat and bowed their heads for a silent blessing on the food. And as they all prayed together, Thad prayed for the baby born too soon, for Lydia's family, and especially for Lydia, too.

God, provide for her… he prayed. And this time, he didn't let his own jealousy stop his prayer. *Even if I can't be her answer.*

Chapter Ten

T had arrived at one on the dot, and she loaded up her cloth bags of precious crocheted toys into the back seat of the truck, then hopped up into the passenger side. The drive to the Greenberg Hospital took forty-five minutes, and she always felt nervous on trips like these. While she knew the client care team appreciated her donations, there was always that shy nervousness about handing over something she'd worked so hard on. But sitting next to Thad was a pleasant distraction from her usual nervousness. They didn't even have to talk about much for the time together to be enjoyable. He had an easy smile when he glanced over at her, and she liked the way he drove with one hand draped over the steering wheel. He looked strong and relaxed.

Lydia had four finished crocheted Noah's Arks complete with animals, and three pairs of lions and lambs that she had designed to lay down side by side like in the Bible passage. She also had several crocheted lambs on their own. *Kinner* seemed to like the lambs a lot—perhaps some deep part of them identifying with a gentle creature that needed love and care. Sometimes she sold these at craft fairs, so she always had a little stash of toys that had a Biblical connection. It wasn't that she saw anything wrong with teddy bears, but the comfort she strove to bring came from a higher Source. She wanted those *kinner* to remember that someone was praying for them.

The hospital was located on the edge of the city. The emergency entrance was bustling as an ambulance unloaded a patient, and Thad circled around to the visitors' parking garage and found a spot there. The garage was chilly and smelled faintly of motor oil—a smell that Lydia could never get used to.

They got out, and the slamming truck door echoed.

"Here, let me help," Thad said. He pulled the three bags out of the back seat, and she accepted one. The other two, Thad carried in one hand. They certainly weren't heavy, just a little awkward.

"Danke," Lydia said. "I feel a little nervous, but they did ask the bishop if we could help. I hope they still want these."

"I'm sure they do," he said. "This time of year is tough for a lot of families, especially those struggling with hospital bills. It will make a difference. I'm sure of it."

"I hope so. I pray when I crochet. My fingers know the work, and my heart can turn to more important things. I pray for the child who will receive the gift, and for *Gott*'s will in their little lives. I assumed these would go to Amish *kinner*, but *Gott* knew better."

Thad's gaze softened. "That's beautiful."

They walked through the chilly cement parking garage, and Thad's fingers brushed against hers. She held her breath and didn't move her hand, and she felt his fingers brush hers again. She looked over at him, and she saw a bit of color in his face as he scooped up her hand.

"Okay?" he asked.

Lydia nodded and she exhaled a shaky sigh. Finally... Was it terrible that it felt this good to have his warm fingers wrapped around hers? He walked slowly next to her, as if he were in no hurry to end this, and while they were in relative privacy, she leaned into his strong arm. If only they could continue this way...

But then they emerged into the bright afternoon sunlight, and she released his hand and took a step away from him. He cast her a smile, and they continued into the hospital side by side. He caught the door for her and she passed in ahead of him.

The lobby smelled faintly of disinfectant, and there was a big sign with arrows directing people to different wings of the hospital. Radiology, Oncology, Emergency, Neonatal... Mary would be here, too, and Lydia hoped to visit her friend, if she could. An old man in slippers and a bathrobe shuffled past the door, a nurse next to him for support.

There was a sign that pointed to the volunteer office, and she glanced over at Thad and gestured in that direction.

"Lead the way," Thad said, but he kept up with her as they headed down the hallway.

Lydia introduced herself and explained that her bishop had asked her to make some toys for the children at the hospital, and she hoped that they were expecting her.

"Miss Speicher, it's a pleasure to see you," the receptionist said. "Yes, we knew you'd be coming. We truly appreciate this. With Christmas coming, the children need some cheering up so badly. And healing is much faster when a child is happy, I can tell you that."

"I'm glad to help," Lydia said. "Here are the toys.

I…I hope they are what the children will like. These are toys that our *kinner* enjoy in our community, but I know Englisher boys and girls have different expectations."

Lydia opened up the bag in her hand and pulled out a Noah's Ark set. She demonstrated how the animals went in and out of the boat and the receptionist beamed.

"This is beautiful!"

"*Danke.* I work hard on them. There are several Noah's Arks, and I have these little lions and lambs… If it would help the families, perhaps you could tell them that I pray for the child while I make these toys, too."

"Those positive thoughts are always helpful," the woman said with a nod.

This woman wasn't a Christian, it would seem. Positive thinking was important in a patient's recovery, Lydia knew, but prayer was something different entirely. Prayer was a connection to the Creator of the universe. An answered prayer was Him reaching down and altering reality for them. That wasn't a positive thought. That was faith. But it didn't seem like the right time to correct theology.

"If I've brought too many, I understand," Lydia said.

"We always need them," the receptionist assured her. "We are so grateful for these little tokens of love."

Lydia smiled. "I'm really glad. These Noah's Arks belong with six little animals each…" And Lydia started to separate out the sets, and the receptionist tucked the animals inside each ark and set them aside. The lions and the lambs were bound together with elastic bands so they wouldn't be separated.

"And these lambs here—" Lydia pulled out the last items, all a little bit bigger "—can be given out separately."

Lydia paused with her hand on the last lamb—a little white-and-black lamb that she'd crocheted last. It had little black hooves and a black face and ears. It was a dear little lamb, but the reason why she didn't relinquish it wasn't because it was a favorite.

"I have a friend here in the hospital," Lydia said. "She just had a baby prematurely, and I had hoped to stop by and see her."

"Of course you need to bring her that!" the receptionist said, seeming to understand immediately. "Miss Speicher, we truly appreciate your generosity. And I hope your friend is doing well."

Lydia gave the woman a grateful smile, and she turned back to see Thad waiting by the door, his eyes cast downward.

"Do you mind if we stop by and see Mary?" Lydia asked softly as they moved back into the hallway.

"Of course not," Thad said. "Especially since we're here. I'm sure she'd appreciate the visit."

"How do we find her?" Lydia slowed her pace. "Someone here would know where she is..."

"She'd probably be up in the maternity wing," Thad said. "I'm sure the nurses up there could point us to the right room."

That sounded logical, and she was grateful for his calmness right now. They stopped in front of the big sign. The maternity section was upstairs on the second floor, so they headed for the elevator. Lydia looked down at the little lamb in her hands. She prayed whenever she crocheted, and she distinctly remembered the prayers she'd said while she'd worked on this last lamb.

Thad didn't take her hand again, but she did lean into

his warm shoulder, and he leaned back just enough that she could feel it like a returned hug.

The elevator doors opened, and Lydia straightened again. They headed out into a bustling maternity ward. Nurses were smiling and there seemed to be a lot of families visiting new mothers. There was an abundance of bouncing gift shop balloons.

"Hi," Lydia said to a passing nurse. "I'm looking for an Amish woman—Mary Schrock."

"Oh yes!" the nurse said. "Her mom and dad have gone to find some supper, so she's alone right now. She's very tired, though, so you'll need to keep your visit short."

"*Yah.* I just wanted to bring her a small gift. We've been praying for her."

"She's in room 209," the nurse said. "But I'll have to ask you to limit your stay to about ten minutes. She needs rest."

"*Danke,*" Lydia said. "I appreciate it."

The room was dim and quiet when Lydia tapped on the door and opened it just a little to look inside. There was only one bed, but she could see that Mary's eyes were open. Her face was pale and puffy, and she looked so unlike herself in that blue-checkered hospital gown and with an IV in her arm.

"Lydia?" Mary said. "Come in."

Lydia came into the room, and Thad stepped inside, too, but he stayed at the door.

"That's Thad Miller. He gave me a ride," Lydia said. He'd done so much more, but this was not the time. Mary gave Thad a nod.

"How are you feeling?" Lydia asked, and she pulled a chair up next to the bed.

"I'm okay," Mary said. "I had my baby. It's a boy. We named him Leonard, after my husband. We'll call him Lenny for short."

"That's really sweet," Lydia said, and tears welled in her eyes. "Oh, Mary. I'm happy for you. And we're all praying for you and little Lenny. Where is he?"

"In the NICU," Mary said. "He's in an incubator. I can visit him whenever I want, but the nurses say I have to rest so I get better. So my parents will help me go see him again when they get back from supper."

Lydia looked down at the little lamb in her hands and she handed it over to Mary.

"I made this for you," Lydia said, emotion stuck in her throat. "I prayed with every stitch, Mary. I prayed for whomever would get this little lamb—for strength and healing, and for *Gott*'s will, and for blessing, and…" She swallowed hard. "All those hundreds of prayers are for you and little Lenny. And I'll keep praying."

Mary reached out and took her hand. "*Danke*, Lydia. It means the world to me."

"How are you feeling?" Lydia asked.

"Tired." Mary smiled faintly. "But happy, too. I can't believe I'm a *mamm*."

"I know! It's wonderful," Lydia said softly. "And I can't wait until you're home again and I can see you in your own kitchen with your baby in your arms."

"Pray for it," Mary said earnestly.

"I am," Lydia whispered.

They talked for another couple of minutes about Christmas plans. Mary would be spending Christmas in the hospital, but her parents would come and she'd spend as much time as she could in the NICU holding her baby. Nothing had turned out the way Mary had planned, but she was happy all the same. With *Gott*'s blessing, the details didn't matter. All that mattered was her little boy's safety.

The nurse tapped on the door and poked her head inside.

"We need to let our mom rest," the nurse said with a smile.

Lydia stood up and gave her friend's hand one last squeeze.

"Merry Christmas, Mary," Lydia said softly.

"Merry Christmas," her friend replied.

Sometimes *Gott* used the humble efforts of a woman with no *boblis* of her own to bless other people's *boblis*, and this time Lydia prayed with an earnest spirit that *Gott* would wrap tiny Lenny in healing, and his mother Mary, too. That his precious life would be preserved, and he'd grow up to be a good, strong man who'd make his mother proud.

As Lydia and Thad got to the elevator, Thad slid an arm around her shoulder, and she tipped her head against him. He didn't say a word, and neither did she. Words weren't needed right now, but his strong presence was a bigger comfort than he would know.

When Thad pulled into the Speichers' drive, he was disappointed the drive home hadn't taken longer. There were a couple of extra buggies parked next to the stable, and two more horses in the corral. The family had visitors, it seemed. This time with Lydia was proving to be precious, and it wouldn't last much longer. Dr. Ted was coming back the next day, and he'd resume his regular duties soon. Things would be different then.

"Dr. Ted comes back tomorrow," Thad said.

"Does he?" Lydia sucked in a wavering breath.

"He texted me and asked if I could meet him for our first appointment," Thad said. "That would be the Knussli farm."

"Can you find it yourself?" Lydia asked, and there was such hope in her voice that he couldn't help but feel his own hope rising, too. Maybe they could have one more drive together tomorrow.

"I, uh—" He didn't want to lie. "I could use some navigation help. We were using back roads with the sleigh, and I think I could find the farm again, but with you along, I'd find it faster."

There. That was the honest truth.

"I'd be happy to show you the way," Lydia said and her gaze locked onto his. "If you want me to."

"I definitely want you to," he said with a short laugh. "Very much. I'll see you in the morning then?"

"I'll be ready." She smiled then, and he reached out and squeezed her hand.

The side door opened, and Lydia's mother appeared. She waved, and two small girls peeked around her skirts. Thad sighed. Privacy was in short supply with an Amish family.

"Those are my nieces," Lydia said, and she cast Thad a grateful smile. "Thank you for taking me to the hospital today. It was so kind of you."

"Of course," he said. "Any time. If you need me, just call. Here—" He dug in his pocket and pulled out a business card.

It wasn't quite so simple for the Amish. She'd have to go to a telephone hut to make the call, but she could still find him. And he'd do whatever he could to help her whenever she needed it.

"Would you like to come inside?" Lydia asked, accepting the card almost reverently.

But this was a family gathering, and Thad wasn't family. They were generous and hospitable, but Thad couldn't keep inserting himself into her private world. It wasn't fair to any of them. The problem was, he'd thoroughly enjoy an evening with Lydia and her family. He'd like to see the similarities between the sisters and chat with her brother-in-law. He'd enjoy it the way a man enjoyed getting to know his girlfriend's family, and that wasn't right. She wasn't his to enjoy that way.

"I'd better get some rest," he said. A flimsy excuse, but it would do.

Lydia seemed to read the hesitation in his face, but she didn't push the issue.

"Well..." Lydia pushed open the door. "I'll see you tomorrow, then."

She got out, and the little girls hopped up and down on the step waiting for her. Lydia bent down and scooped both girls up into a big hug, then disappeared inside.

Thad put the truck into Reverse, and he pulled back out again. He felt oddly sad as he drove back to the bed-and-breakfast. Why did this feel like a goodbye? He was seeing her tomorrow! But he knew just as solidly that this connection with her couldn't last. Her life was here.

Thad's cell phone rang and he picked up the call on speaker. It wasn't a number he recognized.

"Dr. Thad Miller," he said. "How can I help?"

"Dr. Miller, this is Dr. Granger at the Pennsylvania Commercial Dairy Association. I was really impressed to hear about your contribution to curing our sick calves. I wanted to thank you personally."

"You're very welcome," Thad replied. "It was my pleasure. I don't know why the idea occurred to me—mostly we had to do something or lose that first calf."

"Those medications are contraindicative. What was your scientific thought behind the attempt?"

For the next few minutes, Thad talked to the head of the veterinarian team about his decision to use the medications together and why he'd thought it would work. They discussed his studies, and his views for the future in bovine veterinarian care, and when Thad pulled into the Draschel B&B, he parked next to the Beiler buggy and stayed in the truck to finish his conversation.

"Well, we're impressed," Dr. Granger said. "And we have a position open for our team. This would be full-time care of the cattle on five dairy farms. You'd have several veterinarian technicians beneath you to carry out your directions, and you'd be working with five other veterinarians, including Dr. Smythe, as a team. Are you interested in hearing about the salary?"

"Yeah, that definitely interests me," he said.

The number that Dr. Granger quoted him was more than generous. It would make everything easier for Thad, and he suddenly had an image in his mind of an acreage of his own where he could have horses, a nice big dog, and enough land to feel like he could really breathe. But that cost money, and this job would provide it.

"What do you say?" Dr. Granger asked.

And while the yes was on the tip of his tongue, the thought of Lydia held him back. The dairy association was cutting edge, the top vets working together to use the top technology for milk production, and it was perfect. It was ideal. It was everything he'd dreamed of for years, but it was also the direct opposite of this quiet, slow-paced life here. And while he had no logical reason to put off his yes, he couldn't quite bring himself to commit.

"Sir, if you don't mind, I just need a day or two to think it over," Thad said. "I'm excited. This is very generous, but I just need to wrap my brain around it first."

"Of course," Dr. Granger said. "I can give you a couple of days, but we need to fill this spot, and I need to hear back before Christmas."

Christmas was three days away. So don't dillydally. That was what Dr. Granger meant.

"Thank you, sir," Thad said. "I'll get back to you soon."

He hung up the call and opened his heart to God.

Thank you, Lord, he prayed. *This is everything I asked You for. So why doesn't it feel quite right?*

Thad got out of the truck and headed toward the house. There would be some food waiting for him there. But he'd noticed something tonight. When he had the invitation, he hadn't gone in to visit with Lydia's family. And when he was offered it, he hadn't accepted the job of his dreams, either.

What was wrong with him? What was holding him back?

He truly wished he knew.

The next day, Thad picked up Lydia at nine sharp, and they headed out toward the Knussli farm. Lydia was in a subdued mood, and so was Thad. This would be his last ride with her—at least with her as his ride-along navigator.

"Left at the stop sign," Lydia said.

He knew that now, but it still felt nice to have her here.

"How was your visit with your sister and her family?" Thad asked.

"It was wonderful." She smiled. "We're sending a box of little gifts to my brother's family in the city. I don't know if his *kinner* enjoy the practical things our *kinner* enjoy here, but we want them to know that they're loved, all the same."

"I'm sure they'll appreciate it," he said.

"I hope so."

They went around the corner and continued up the road, the horse's breath clouding in the cold winter air.

"I was offered a job at the Pennsylvania Commercial Dairy Association," Thad said.

Lydia's face whipped toward him. "Is that good for you?"

"I'm not sure," he admitted. "It's good for my career. It's good for my bank account, too. But something is holding me back."

"What?" she asked.

"I'm not sure. I was hoping you might know." He cast her a hopeful look.

She gave him a rueful smile. "I can't read your mind, Thad."

"But you do have wonderful insights," he said. "I was actually looking forward to talking it over with you."

"Maybe it's a good job, a good opportunity, and a good place to work, but not what *Gott* has for you," she suggested.

That was the kind of insight he'd been hoping for. Was this wonderful in many ways, but just not God's will?

"That might be the case," Thad agreed. "Or I'm just scared of something new. It's all very cutting edge. It's the newest technology. Sometimes new, progressive things can be intimidating to a Beachy Amish man like me."

Lydia sobered. "As an Amish woman, that sounds dangerous to my ear."

It was the same for him…in a way. But at the same time it sounded exciting. They could use technology like that in their workplaces for the Beachy Amish. He wouldn't be breaking any rules in his faith community.

"Would it be against the rules here?" he asked.

Lydia was silent for a moment, her lips pressed together. "*Yah*. I believe so."

That's what he thought. Was that what was holding him back—that look on her face? He'd known this would be far too fancy for Lydia, and quite frankly, it shouldn't matter! She wasn't his wife. She wasn't even his girl-friend. But she mattered to him rather deeply.

"I'm going to come back and visit you," Thad said. He did want to see her again.

"Do you mean you'll visit my family?" she asked.

"I can't visit you?" he asked, looking over at her. He'd been hoping to take her out for a drive—get some time alone with her again. Talk more deeply alone.

"It would be more proper if you visited my parents, too," she said. "Otherwise, my community would think you were courting me."

Right. The proprieties. His heart sank. If a man wanted one-on-one time with a woman, he'd better make his intentions clear, and simply missing her wasn't good enough.

"Then I'll visit your family," he amended. "As long as I get to see you again."

Lydia smiled at that, but it didn't feel like enough for him. The rest of the ride was quiet, the heat pumping into the cab of the truck. Lydia sat with her hands clasped in her lap, so he didn't even have the chance to hold her hand, either. And when they crested the hill and came down toward the Knussli farm, instead of feeling the joy of that gorgeous scene rolling out in front of him, he felt a tightness in his chest that he knew was connected to the woman beside him. He'd miss her more than he should.

They pulled into the Knussli drive, and Thad spotted Dr. Ted's truck parked beside the house. Adel Knussli stood on the step with her baby on one hip, a blanket bundled around the little guy, and she waved when she spotted Lydia in the truck.

"Do you want to see me?" Thad asked. Because that was what he needed to know.

"Do I want to?" Lydia asked, turning toward him. "Of course I *want* to. It's just..."

Dr. Ted was looking in their direction now, too, and Lydia's words evaporated. They had an audience now, and while the rumbling engine would keep their words private, it was awkward being watched this way.

"Maybe we should talk about this after," Thad said, turning off the truck.

Lydia nodded. "I agree. Since Dr. Ted is here to help you, maybe I'll go inside and chat with Adel."

The men and the women—they were separate worlds in his Beachy Amish congregation, but even more so with the Old Order. And just for once, he wished it wasn't so, because he longed for a little more time with her. But this was life, and maybe it was even good for him. He shouldn't be toying with emotions this strong, and those traditions were like a fence to protect more than reputations. It protected vulnerable hearts, too.

Thad and Lydia got out of the truck, and Lydia headed up to the house, while Dr. Ted came tramping through the snow toward him.

Thad shook the older man's hand firmly.

"Good to see you," Thad said. "How was your trip?"

"Oh, it was wonderful," Dr. Ted said. "I have two brand new granddaughters, and they are just beautiful. Strong and healthy, and I sat there and held them both at the same time for a solid week. I loved every second of it."

"That's really great," Thad said.

"Which brings me to why I wanted to talk with you," Dr. Ted said. "Why don't we head out to the barn?"

Lydia headed toward the house and the women disappeared inside together. Thad fell in beside the older veterinarian and the snow crunched underfoot.

"I made a decision while I was away. I'm going to be slowing down," Dr. Ted said. "I want to visit my grandkids more often, and my wife is tired of all my long hours. It's time for me to scale back a bit."

"That's understandable," Thad said. "You've worked hard and you deserve the rest."

"I don't need an assistant so much as I need someone to take over for me," Ted said, stopping and turning to face Thad. "I like you. I respect your work ethic, and the people around here seem to like you, too. I've been asking around since I got back yesterday. This worked out as well as I'd hoped."

"Oh?" Thad felt his heart lift just a bit.

"I want you to take over," Ted said. "I'm going to step

back, and I want to put you on salary to take over my regular workload. I'd help out in busy times, but other than that, I'd take care of the clinic and slow down. When you're ready to buy me out, you let me know. How does that sound?"

Thad's heart was hammering hard. "This is my second offer in two days," he admitted.

"Who else offered you a job?" Ted demanded, sounding a little offended.

When Thad explained, the older man sighed. "This is a different kind of offer. This is working with small farms and local people. It's hard work, but it's also a chance to run your own practice. I'll let you buy me out for a fair deal. It would all be yours. You'd call the shots, be your own boss. But I don't make the kind of money an outfit like that can offer. I'll tell you that plainly."

"Still, it is very tempting," Thad said. "And I can definitely see how money isn't everything in a choice like this."

"You'll need time to think about it," Ted assumed.

"I think I will," Thad agreed. "But I'm really grateful for the offer. Can you give me a couple of days to mull it over? I'll tell you by Christmas, if that's okay."

"That's fine by me," Ted said.

They started walking again, and as they headed up toward the barn, the door opened and Jake Knussli waved to them. Thad needed some time to think this over, but more than that, he wanted Lydia's opinion. She had a way of keeping his boots on the ground, and he needed that right now more than anything.

Chapter Eleven

Lydia sat at Adel's kitchen table with a cup of hot tea in front of her and baby in her lap. She had pushed away from the table to keep the tea out of reach, and he stuck his tongue out of his mouth, his wide eyes shining with happiness. Adel's older son Samuel was playing with a bowling set in the living room—the pins crashing loudly every time they knocked over. Adel looked in the direction of the noise.

"Samuel, I want you to pick that up and put it away," she called.

Lydia widened her eyes and made a face for little Levi, who babbled in delight.

"Just a minute," Adel said, and she picked up a wooden crate and carried it into the other room. There was the soft murmur of her voice, and then she returned.

"Now, let's talk about adult business," Adel said. "Is it just me, or are you and that Beachy Amish veterinarian getting closer?"

From the living room there was the banging sound of pins going into the crate one by one. Samuel was a little boy and the noise seemed to bring him joy.

"Me and Thad?" Lydia asked, ignoring the clatter.

"No, we're—" But that sounded an awful lot like a lie to Lydia, and she felt her face heat. "*Yah*, we are."

"And?" Adel asked, pulling up a chair. She reached for her baby and tucked him into her lap neatly.

"We shouldn't be!" Lydia said. "He's Beachy Amish. He drives a truck, he wears that cowboy-style hat, and he…he… He's not Old Order."

Adel sighed. "I'd hoped that since he was using a buggy for a while, he might have changed his mind on that?"

"It's not so easy for people to adopt our way of life, Adel," Lydia said. "I've seen one of the places where Thad was working. It's…it's so shiny and computerized, and…and…fancy. Adel, it's just the fanciest barn I've seen in my life. And they offered him a job. It's a good job—very good for him—and I think he'll take it."

"Close by, but miles apart," Adel murmured.

"*Yah*, exactly. I thought my father was overreacting about how different the Beachy Amish are, but they're so different. They're almost like Englishers. They use electricity in their homes, and they use electric sewing machines, and…" She couldn't think of anything else because she hadn't heard of much besides that, but it was enough.

"But you have feelings for him," Adel said.

"It doesn't matter."

"I agree that it might not matter when it comes to whether or not you have a future with Thad, but your feelings do matter," Adel said. "If you just push them down and ignore them, they will find a way back up again."

Lydia nodded. "I do care for him. I've been praying that *Gott* will bring me a man very much like him. Maybe that's what *Gott* was trying to show me."

Adel nodded. "Maybe. I can look around at other communities, write some letters…"

Lydia felt a knot in her throat. "Not yet, Adel. Maybe later on."

But wasn't that what she wanted—a husband of her own? Wasn't that her own personal goal? Why couldn't she let their matchmaker do her job and find her a proper Old Order Amish match?

Lydia and Adel talked about other things, like Mary and her premature son in the hospital, and about Claire and Joel who were expecting another baby, about Naomi and Mose and their planned Christmas visit. They chatted about Delia and her new husband Elias, who were planning Delia's eldest son's wedding now, right on the heels of their own. And then there was Verna, who had recently agreed to teach a single mothers' knitting class at the community center. So many updates on their friends to be happy for, and to pray for, too. It was better than feeling sorry for herself.

When Samuel finished cleaning up his bowling pins, he came into the kitchen and chattered at Lydia about his bowling pins, and about a picture book he liked a lot, and about the snow outside and how his *daet* wouldn't let him dig a hole in a snowdrift to play like he was a bear hibernating because it could be dangerous. One story turned into another, and the time slipped away until they heard the men's voices outside.

"Looks like they're finished," Adel said, looking out the window.

Lydia joined Adel at the window and looked out at

Thad standing there with Dr. Ted and Jake. They were chatting like men did, and Thad stood there with his weight shifted onto one leg, and somehow the sight of him so relaxed with the men gave her heart a squeeze. He seemed to feel her gaze, because he turned and when he saw her, a smile split his face.

"He feels it, too," Adel murmured.

Lydia pretended not to hear, and she headed for the door and stepped back into her boots. She pulled her thick shawl around her shoulders, and headed outside. Thad said his goodbyes to the men and stepped away from them, waiting for Lydia before he walked with her to his truck.

"I'll bring you home," he said.

"Danke," she murmured.

Thad opened the truck door for her, and Lydia got up inside. She had to admit that she was grateful for the warmth of the truck. A buggy was considerably colder in the middle of winter. Thad hopped up and started the truck, the heat turning back on and pumping onto Lydia's legs.

Thad waved to Dr. Ted and Jake, and put the truck into Reverse. He seemed like he was in a hurry to get away, and she did up her seat belt as they headed up the drive toward the road.

"Did you have a good visit?" Thad asked. He sounded distracted, though.

"Yah, it was very nice," she said. "Why do you sound almost strangled?"

"Do I?" He shot her a rueful smile. "I guess I do. I actually wanted to talk something over with you."

"The job offer, you mean?" she asked.

"There's been another one," he said.

"Another job offer?"

"Dr. Ted has an interesting proposal for me." He blew out a breath. "And I wanted to hear what you thought about it."

His tone was low and quiet, just for her. And if he were Old Order, she'd think he was asking her because she might be a part of that life he was planning.

"It doesn't matter what I think, does it?" she asked, and her voice sounded too harsh, somehow, and she didn't mean to. It was just how it came out.

"It matters to me," he said. He sounded hurt.

"Why ask me, though?" Lydia smoothed her hands down her thighs.

"Because I like how you think."

It was an unexpected compliment and she blinked over at him. "But I'm not Beachy Amish."

"No, and I'm not asking you as someone who is Old Order, either. I'm asking you as my...friend."

Friend. They were more than friends—she knew that for a fact. "Friend" sounded like a backtrack almost, but she couldn't blame him, either. They couldn't officially be anything more, and that fact stung.

"I'm sure you have friends who have known you longer," she said.

"I do," he said, and he cast her a frustrated look. "But somehow I don't care about their opinions. I care about yours."

"So what are your choices?" she asked with a sigh.

"A better-paying job with a top commercial dairy association," he said, "or a chance at owning my own practice and working with families here in the Redemption area."

Being closer still, working here in the community...

"Would...would you come to Service Sunday?" she asked.

"If you asked me."

Her heartbeat sped up, but attending service meant nothing if he wasn't Old Order. His life would continue and every second Sunday he'd come and associate. It wasn't enough, and she knew it. It was playing with fire, and her heart was the dry tinder.

"So it's a better-paying job that might not last for a lifetime," she said, trying to pull things back to the question at hand, "or a lower-paying job that might turn into owning your own practice for life."

"Yes, that's it." His eyes were locked on the road.

"And you want me to help you choose?" she asked.

"Yes."

She was silent.

"Do you have any thoughts on the matter?" he asked. "As in...you want me to be closer by? Would you like me to work in the community here?"

"Do *you* want to be closer by?" she asked, exasperated. "This is about you, Thad! What do you want? Do you want to be near *me*?"

"Of course I do!" he shot back. "I want to see you! I want to visit you."

"Why?" she demanded, turning a fiery gaze on him. Because she didn't know why he was doing this! Why was he focused on her this way? Why was he making her heart skip beats and making her long for him this way? It wasn't fair!

"Because I love you!" Thad retorted, the muscle along his jawline tensing. "Okay? I love you. I want to see you. That's how things stand for me."

Thad hadn't meant to say that, and his breath caught in his chest. Why had he said that? It was true, but not everything true needed to be spoken out loud!

"What?" Lydia breathed.

Thad looked over to find Lydia staring at him, her face white. Had he scared her? Had he offended her? He heaved a miserable sigh.

"I'm sorry I told you that," he said, softening his tone. "I shouldn't have. I know I'm not the kind of man for you."

"You...love me?"

Thad looked over at her as he slowed the truck for a stop sign. "Very much."

"Why would you be sorry?" she asked.

"Because—" He wasn't sure he wanted to say this, but since he'd already blurted out the worst... "Because I think this might be one-sided. I think I fell for you, and you're now in a really awkward position of having to tell me—"

"I love you, too." Lydia's words seemed to come out in a rush, and he pressed the brake, bringing them to a complete stop. There was no one behind them on the road and he reached over and caught her hand.

"You know how I promised I wouldn't kiss you unless you asked me to?" he asked, his heart hammering in his chest.

She nodded.

"Would you mind asking for that kiss?" he asked.

A smile touched her lips. "I'm too shy to say that, Thad…"

And he'd made a promise, so he didn't lean in and take that kiss he wanted so badly. He held her hand, though, and he pulled around the corner onto her road. They were so close to her place, too close. He needed more time to sort this out, because he hadn't expected her to admit to loving him, and now that she had, he needed to know where he stood with her.

"So you love me, and I love you," he said, keeping the truck moving as slowly as possible down the gravel road.

She didn't answer, but her hand tightened on his.

"Is there any hope for us?" he asked, but even as the words came out, he doubted there was. He knew what stood between them.

"You're kind and smart, and you care about others," she said quietly, pulling her fingers free of his. "You're a man of faith, too, even if it's not the right faith for me… But you're a good man, Thad."

She had a really awful way of letting a guy down, because everything she said about him made him feel like there might be hope.

"I'm an Amish Christian," he said.

"Thad…"

She didn't have to say more. She was Old Order, and he wasn't. She lived so much more simply than he had ever experienced before. He was a veterinarian who relied upon science and technology to help the animals in his care, and his future lay in that direction. Whichever job he took, they'd still be a world apart.

"I know," he said. "You don't have to explain all over again."

He pulled up to the Speicher drive, and he could feel the time slipping away from them.

"I just want you to know that you're a beautiful woman," he said, his voice tight. "And that you're incredible. You're sweet, and pretty, and insightful, and… I know someone will marry you and you'll make him a wonderful wife. And I'll be jealous of him because it won't be me. But I want you to know."

"Oh, Thad…" Tears choked her voice. "I wish there were a way. I'll pray that *Gott* bless you and keep you and give you a better woman than me."

He turned into the drive. She was saying no, but even in turning a man's heart away, she was kind.

"That's not possible to find a better woman," he said.

There was a pickup truck parked next to the buggy already, and he recognized it as her brother's vehicle. This family had enough drama without outsiders, and he didn't need to add to it.

Thad pulled to a stop on the other side of the buggy, and he looked over at Lydia.

"If things were different…" she whispered.

"I know." He nodded, swallowing against the knot in his throat. "I feel the same way. If things were different, I'd be pursuing more with you. A lot more."

Lydia looked up at him, and he reached up and touched her soft cheek. Life was so cruel that he'd meet a woman like Lydia, and she'd be everything his heart desired, and there would still be a wall between them. But he knew that when he came out to Old Order Amish country. He knew that no matter how special a woman might be, she'd be off-limits to him. This wasn't a surprise, but it still hurt in a part of his heart that had never ached like this before.

The side door to the house opened and Art looked out. Her father must have been back at home for lunch. He wasn't wearing his hat, and he stood in shirt sleeves and suspenders. It was cold out. She'd better get inside. This was her father's way of hurrying her out of his vehicle.

Lydia looked toward her father, too, then back at Thad.

"I'm sorry." Tears welled in her eyes.

"Go," he said, swallowing hard. "I'll see you later. I'll…let you know what job I take. If you want me to."

She nodded mutely, then pushed open the door. She hopped out and slammed it shut again.

He'd never gotten her advice on which job to take, he realized. But did it matter anymore? Feeling like he did about her, he should probably take the job as far from her as possible, because bumping into her was going to hurt. And while he knew she'd marry another man, he didn't want to see it. He'd loved her first.

When Thad arrived back at the B&B, his heart was heavy. How was he supposed to make a decision like this that would affect the trajectory of his whole career while he was utterly heartbroken?

Lord, I know I can't be with Lydia. I know that…but I can't stop thinking about her. Please give me some clarity. I have such an important decision to make.

And before Christmas, too. He parked next to the stable and sat in his truck for a couple of minutes, watching the horses in the corral. Sometimes he wished he could live this simple life—just be a man doing a job in order to provide for the woman he loved… But it wasn't so simple.

His phone pinged. It was a text from Ethan, telling him that he'd love to work with him. And it would be nice to work with a friend, especially in such a top-rung organization. This was the kind of job he'd been dreaming of since boyhood—the kind that would validate him, and prove that he was worthy of more acceptance than he'd ever received as just plain old Thad.

This was the no-brainer choice. This was the job that seemed like a blessing dropped in his lap. This was the kind of position he'd been afraid to even pray for!

So what was holding him back from just accepting it and saying "*danke*"?

Not "*danke*."

"Thank you." Funny how the Pennsylvania Dutch slipped through his thoughts, even at a time like this. But Thad was not Old Order, and he couldn't pretend that he was.

The stable door opened and Joel Beiler came outside. He gave Thad a wave, and Thad sighed. He'd been wanting advice, hadn't he? He'd been asking too much of Lydia. Maybe it was time to ask someone else.

Thad pushed open his door and hopped out into the snow.

"Hello," Joel said. "If you're hungry, I'm pretty sure my wife has lunch on."

"I'm not really hungry," Thad said. "I'm actually trying to sort out a job offer situation, and I need to make up my mind rather quickly. I wonder if I could just bounce it off of you?"

"Of course," Joel said.

"Okay…" Suddenly Thad was feeling foolish for even needing the sounding board. He felt like he knew what answer he'd get. "I have two offers. One is for a top-rate dairy corporation and I'd be part of a veterinarian team. Good pay, and lots of respect. It would be impressive on my résumé."

"Congratulations," Joel said. "And the other one?"

"Less pay. More physical labor. And I'd have the chance to own my own practice at the end of it."

Joel's eyebrows went up. "If it were me, I'd choose the second one."

"Really?" Thad hadn't expected that. Or maybe he should have. This was an Old Order Amish man, after all.

"I have a few reasons," Joel said. "First of all, hard physical labor is good for a man. It tires you out at the end of a day, and leaves you feeling like you accomplished something. Secondly, money isn't everything. It never was, and it never will be. Thirdly, you've got a chance of owning your own practice? That's freedom. That's success in these parts, too. I'd take the second option."

But the second option came with seeing Lydia around, too. It came with being close enough to her Old Order world that he could peek in and tear the wound open all over again.

"I take it I didn't give you the answer you wanted," Joel said after a beat of silence.

"I don't know what answer I wanted, honestly," Thad said. "But maybe I wanted the excuse to take the better paying, more exciting job. What would you say if I told you that I could help more people, cure more animals, with more technology available to me? That first job gives me the chance to make a big impact."

"Well…" Joel sucked in a deep breath and his gaze moved over the corral, then beyond it to the field. "You're talking about where you can do more good, am I right?"

"Exactly."

"I'm of the opinion that sometimes more good is done inside of a man than outside of him."

Thad rubbed a hand over the faint stubble on his chin.

"What does Lydia think?" Joel asked.

"Why do you ask that?" Thad asked cautiously.

"There's something between you, isn't there?" Joel asked. "I mean…my wife has been talking about it. The women all seem to sense something there between you. Are they wrong?"

"No, they're right…" Thad sighed. "But I'm not Old Order, and she's not Beachy. We're just…too different. And we know it. Don't worry, there's no need to talk sense into me. Lydia is perfectly safe from me."

"I'm sorry," Joel said. "I know what heartbreak feels like."

"Yeah?"

"The road that led to my wife Claire was a twisting, turning, difficult road. I didn't think I'd ever get to marry her, but *Gott* had other plans."

"I'm happy for you," Thad said. "Sincerely." And that lump came back to his throat.

There was no way he could face lunch in a kitchen with this couple and their cute children. He'd have to pretend that he was fine, and he wasn't. His heart was literally sore in his chest, and he now felt more confused than before.

He had a choice to make, and there was only one answer he needed. It had to come from above.

"Look, I'm not going to stay for lunch," Thad said. "Thank your wife, though."

"Sure," Joel said with a nod, and he could see in the other man's face that he understood more than Thad probably liked. "But if you get hungry, we always have food."

They were kind people, and while Joel's journey to his wife might have been a difficult one, Thad doubted it was as impossible as the gorge between himself and Lydia.

He'd been a fool to let himself fall in love with her. But then...had there been a choice?

Chapter Twelve

Lydia stood at the kitchen counter peeling potatoes. Her brother Paul was at the kitchen table with their *daet*, talking about some theological differences. It was an on-going debate between father and son. *Daet* would never give up on his Amish beliefs, and Lydia was grateful for that. Paul was forever trying to chip a hole in *Daet*'s views, and while Lydia could see how much it annoyed *Daet*, Art Speicher didn't ever snap.

Janet had come along this time, and she was helping in the kitchen. She wore a pair of snug-fitting blue jeans and a colorful Christmas sweater that had snowmen and snowflakes on a background of white—she was as different from their Amish ways as it was possible to be. But Janet loved Paul, and she was his wife. Her blonde hair fell in waves around her face, and she wore a touch of makeup that stood out rather glaringly in their plain kitchen. But Lydia was glad her sister-in-law had come along this time. Different or not, she was part of the family, and when she didn't come with Paul, it only worried Lydia about the state of their marriage.

"Paul, do we have to argue?" Art asked. "We could just…visit. Tell me about Liam. I know he was working and couldn't come along. But how is school going? What are his plans for the future?"

Lydia's mind wasn't on the update about her nephew, though. She glanced toward the window. Snow had started falling again and swirled lazily against the glass.

"Lydia, you'll peel that potato into a marble," her mother said with a laugh, and Lydia realized she was doing just that. She dropped it into the pot and picked up another potato.

"Are you all right?" Janet asked.

"I'm fine." It was a lie, and it felt wrong coming out of her mouth. "I have other things I'm thinking about," she amended. "It's okay."

"What's the matter?" Willa asked.

"It's the Beachy veterinarian, isn't it?" Art asked with a sigh. "What did he do? I can have the bishop speak with him. He doesn't know our ways. He's…just so Beachy."

Great, now the whole family was involved. This was the last thing she needed. Her broken heart was embarrassing enough.

"He didn't do anything wrong." Lydia felt her throat tighten, and she put down the peeler. Tears were rising, and she wasn't going to talk about this in the kitchen as if it was idle chatter. She'd given a man her heart, and she knew there was no future between them.

"Did he offend you?" Willa asked. "Dear, you can't expect someone so different to understand our ways. You might have to explain some things to him for the next time you help him navigate."

"There won't be a next time," she said, swallowing hard. "Dr. Ted is back."

"Oh…"

"She loves him," Paul said.

"Oh?" Janet asked, and she came up next to Lydia and put a gentle hand on her arm. "Do you love him?"

"She doesn't!" Willa said. "She's just helping." But then her mother looked at her more closely, and her face fell. "Oh, Lydia. You fell for him?"

"I didn't mean to!" Lydia said, and she wiped a tear off her cheek. "Don't worry, I know how things stand. He's not Old Order. I am. Our lives cannot connect—not that way. I understand it very well. I'll just need time to make my peace with it."

"Why should you?" Paul demanded.

"Paul…" Janet said. "Stop pestering her. You understand perfectly well. She isn't you. And she isn't me. Lydia knows her own heart."

Lydia gave her sister-in-law a grateful look. Janet should come more often when Paul visited—she actually seemed to be a balancing effect on her brother.

"I'm not giving up my faith, Paul," Lydia said. "You did. You left it all. Fine! Okay? But I'm not leaving the Old Order life!"

"I think you're being a coward," Paul replied.

"Paul!" both her parents said together.

"No one else will say it, but I will!" Paul retorted. "You believe in this life. I get it. But you don't want to live your life unmarried, either. And that's fair, Lydia! You're allowed to want to get married and have your own home. You don't have to pretend this is enough for you if it isn't!"

That was Paul—always saying the things that slipped under her armor and stabbed the deepest. He was married with a family of his own—did he have to push at her like this?

"Did I say it's enough?" Lydia retorted. "It's not! I love our parents, but I want marriage! But if I don't meet a man I can marry, what am I supposed to do about that?"

"You met a man you fell in love with," Paul countered. "And I can tell you, finding someone who makes you feel that much doesn't come around very often. When I met Janet, I knew she was once in a lifetime. I knew it! That's why when you get married you stand by that person. You fight for your marriage. Not because of a rule. Not because you would be shunned if you didn't, but because you know how precious that connection is."

Janet shot Paul a misty smile.

"Maybe there's a way," Janet said quietly. "Paul is right about this kind of love coming around rather rarely."

"He's not from our faith," Willa interjected. "Paul, you can pretend you don't understand all you want, but we raised you to this life. Stop making this harder than it needs to be for your sister."

"*Mamm*, you're holding her back!" Paul said.

"Watch how you speak to your mother!" Art said, raising his voice.

"They are not holding me back!" Lydia said. "What would you have me do, Paul? Say it plainly. You want me to leave the faith."

"I didn't say that." Paul sighed.

Janet crossed the kitchen and stopped at Lydia's crochet bag. It gaped open and Janet bent down and pulled out a newly finished lamb.

"I remember you telling me years ago that when you

crochet these stuffed animals, you pray with every stitch, for the child who will receive it," Janet said, her quiet voice coming clearly through the men's raised voices as they argued.

"I still do," Lydia replied. "I pray that *Gott* will do wonderful things for the person who receives it. I pray for blessing on them, whoever they might be."

The men fell silent.

"And when you pray, you believe that *Gott* will move, right?" Janet asked.

"*Yah.* Of course I do," Lydia said earnestly. If she didn't, she'd be wasting her time.

"Can I have this?" Janet asked.

"What?" Lydia wiped at her cheek.

"Can I have this lamb?" she asked.

"*Yah*, of course." She sucked in a shaky breath.

Janet crossed the kitchen and held it out to her. "Good. So this is now my lamb, crocheted by Lydia Speicher. And I'm giving it to you. So all those prayers—how many, a hundred? A thousand? They're for you now. All those prayers for blessing, and guidance, and answers, and solutions, and bravery."

Lydia accepted the little lamb wordlessly.

"God can do the same things for you that He does for others," Janet said earnestly. "I don't know how He'll work it out for you, but I believe in a God of solutions."

Lydia stared at her sister-in-law mutely. She couldn't disagree…but dare she hope?

"I don't know why you're giving up on him," Paul added. He looked back at their parents. "Why are you all giving up?"

There was silence, then, and Lydia looked toward that

falling snow again. Was there any hope for a future with Thad? Was there any possibility?

"I don't see how it could possibly work," Lydia admitted.

"I do see a solution," Paul said. "I see two, actually. One you won't like, and the other isn't very likely to happen."

"What are they?" Lydia asked. Because with prayer, likeliness didn't matter.

"Either you become Beachy Amish," Paul said, "or he becomes Old Order."

Would she be willing to step back from the Old Order ways and join Thad in his Beachy Amish faith? She was tempted—ever so tempted—but her conscience kept stopping her. She couldn't choose love and give up on what she was certain was *Gott*'s path for her life. She couldn't choose love over *Gott*!

"Sometimes, *Gott* parts the Red Sea," Willa said.

Lydia looked over at her mother, surprised.

"Well, it's true," Willa said. "We don't see a way, but I refuse to allow my fence-jumping son to have more faith than I do."

Art grunted at that, and Paul rolled his eyes.

"You think there's hope?" Lydia asked her mother.

"*Gott* specializes in the impossible," Willa replied. "I don't know what *Gott* will do. I don't know where He will lead you in your lifetime, but I won't stand in the way, either. Trying to block *Gott* is a very dangerous position to take."

"Amen," Janet murmured, and Willa gave her daughter-in-law a squeeze on her way past her.

"Now, Art, if that Beachy Amish man comes with

an open heart and honest curiosity about our faith, are you willing to welcome him?" Willa asked her husband.

"He'd have to become Old Order!" Art said. "He'd have to be properly baptized before he married our daughter. He'd have to—"

"That's a yes?" Willa asked.

Art nodded. "That's a yes."

Paul crossed his arms over his chest and exchanged a smile with his wife. "If he loves you, Lydia, I don't think he'll give up that easily. I guess we'll see what happens. Did you want to call him?"

Paul pulled his cell phone out of his pocket. Lydia did have his phone number on that business card, but she didn't want to take that step. Not yet.

"No," Lydia said. "I have to pray on it. And if he does love me like he says, then he won't expect me to call him on the phone. He'll do it properly and come see me. He'll face *Daet* and *Mamm*."

Paul shrugged. "All right, then. If you want to call me and talk, Lydia, I'll always take your call. Okay? You're my sister. And I promise I won't try to talk you out of being Old Order, but I'll listen."

"Or he could pass the phone to me," Janet said, giving Lydia an affectionate nudge. "I'd love to chat with you, too."

"Danke." Lydia's lips wobbled.

Lydia needed solitude and some space to pray. Her fence-jumping brother, as her mother called him, was full of surprises today, and she had to wonder if *Gott* had been working there. She was also especially grateful for her Englisher sister-in-law who seemed to have more wisdom about her than Lydia had ever given her credit for.

Is there any solution for me? she prayed silently. *I love him,* Gott. *I love him so much! Is there any hope for a life that will please You with Thad Miller?*

Amish farmland slipped past Thad's truck as he rumbled over the unpaved roads. Thad wasn't sure where he was driving to…he needed to think. That was all he knew, and somehow these wide open spaces were calling to him. He had two job offers and all he could think about was Lydia. But he needed to be rational! He needed a job, and he needed to be able to provide for himself. She knew what she wanted, and it wasn't him! What was he supposed to do with that?

His chest ached with suppressed emotion. He didn't want to cry about this, although he felt like that was the only thing that would relieve the pressure building up inside of him. He was a grown man. He knew the chance he had taken, and he'd known that he had very little chance of a future with her. He'd shot his shot, so to speak. That should be comforting in itself, shouldn't it? He'd taken a risk, told her how he felt, and it had all turned out exactly how he'd expected it to.

"So, why does this hurt so much, Lord?" he prayed aloud.

He was starting to know these back roads rather well, and he recognized the Lapp farm ahead. Nathan looked like he was fixing a fence with his son standing next to him holding a mittened handful of nails. The sound of hammer against wood echoed across the rolling farmland.

He'd given Bobli that dose of medication the last time he'd visited this farm, and they'd never called him back.

That either meant that the calf hadn't made it, or she'd made a full recovery. And he wanted to know.

He slowed to a stop on the side of the road and turned on his hazard lights. Then he hopped out into the chill and slammed the door shut after him. Nathan had stopped hammering and gave him a nod.

"Good afternoon, Doc," Nathan said. "How are you?"

"I'm doing okay," he replied. "I just wanted to see how the calf is doing."

"Bobli is better!" Jonathan piped up. "She's eating now, and she's drinking, and she's still got to gain some weight my *daet* says, but she's better now!"

Thad felt a rush of relief. "Good. Good, I'm so glad to hear that."

"We stayed up with her all night when you left," Jonathan said. "My *daet* said that if I was going to stay up, then he was, too. And we did it together, right, *Daet*? We watched her, and we kept her warm, and *Daet* even plugged the heater into the generator because it was an emergency."

"Now, son…" Nathan said.

The boy was chattering, but Thad was touched. Nathan wasn't quite so stern and cold as he appeared, it seemed. He'd stayed up all night with his son and an ailing calf.

"It's okay," Thad said. "You gave up your sleep? Did you sleep at all during the day?"

"When?" Nathan spread his hands. "When Jonathan was a baby, I went on very little sleep. He'd wake us up four times a night, and I'd go back out and work all day. So one sleepless night again wasn't going to kill me.

And if my wife has another child, I'll have sleepless nights again."

"You're a good father," Thad said.

Nathan smiled. *"Danke."* He paused. "Jonathan, run back to the house and ask your *mamm* for a jar of her strawberry jam for Dr. Miller, would you? It's our Christmas gift to you."

"Okay, *Daet*." Jonathan handed the nails back to his father, shaking them out of his knitted mittens carefully. Then he headed off across the snow toward the house in the distance.

"I wanted to talk to you alone, without little ears present," Nathan said with an apologetic smile. "The jam is still for you, of course, but I don't want to tell an untruth."

"Oh?" Thad met the man's steady gaze.

"I thought that Bobli would die. I didn't think there was any hope, and I'd only called you in because my son wouldn't have forgiven me if I hadn't," Nathan said. "And when you came with that first dose of medication, I thought it would be a waste of money, but I did it. For my boy." The Amish man rubbed a gloved hand over his beard. "And I was frustrated with you for giving my son hope again. I'd expected to have to comfort him through a difficult loss in his young life and to teach him that family would be there for him even through heartbreak. Instead, I showed him that while he hoped and prayed, I'd stand behind him. Even when I didn't have the faith of a child."

"There is depth to this life, isn't there?" Thad said thoughtfully.

"Yah, I suppose that's a good way to describe it," Na-

than said. "I don't know anything else, so I might not be the best person to explain the differences, but we believe that a slower pace and harder work build a person's character differently. We are looking for a bedrock foundation here. I don't want to offend, but I think that a lot of other people are building on something less solid."

Something less solid like trying to prove himself to the boys in his youth who hadn't accepted him, trying to prove himself better than them now in his adult years as if that could soothe the pain from his boyhood. What if he stopped trying to clamber higher?

"Do you ever struggle with being so different from the rest of the state, the rest of the country?" Thad asked. "I'm asking you because I think you'll give me an honest answer. Man to man."

"I might not be the right person to ask," Nathan replied. "I was always a bit different from everyone else when I was young. I thought differently. My sense of humor was different. I didn't settle in like the other boys did."

Thad straightened. "Really? I was the same."

"So you understand," Nathan replied.

"All too well. I was on the outside a lot."

Nathan nodded. "Well, our way of life isn't about others. I mean, it's about helping our neighbor and being a community, *yah*. But deep down—" he thumped his chest "—in here, it's about doing things the right way. It really boils down to some very basic principles of honesty, hard work, and personal integrity. It's about laying down in our beds at night and knowing we are right with *Gott* above. And to be right with *Gott*, we must be right with our neighbor. We must help him, support him, be generous with him and forgive him. It isn't about what our neighbor thinks of us or how he treats us. It's about how we think, and how we treat him. That's something in my control."

Thad was silent, his mind moving over this description. It was a life built on a solid foundation. And there was wisdom there. Maybe he didn't need to prove his worth so much as he simply needed to live it out. Such a simple solution, such a simple way of life—and yet a hard one, too. It was the kind of discipline that took a lifetime to master, and yet would have such rich rewards.

"It's Christmastime," Nathan went on. "I think this season comes down to the same things. *Gott* chose Joseph to take care of Mary, to provide for her, and to be a good *daet* to His son, Jesus. He chose a man who He could trust to be a man! That's the job we all have, isn't it? We love our women, we provide for them, and we strive to be good fathers. It's quite basic, but very satisfying."

Up until this point Thad thought there were two choices ahead of him, but there were three. He could take the job with the dairy association, he could take the job with Dr. Ted, or he had a third option—he could take the job with Dr. Ted and join the Old Amish church with Lydia at his side.

But could he make that sacrifice—live a harder way of life in order to embrace those deeper, more difficult lessons?

"Would you like to come see Bobli?" Nathan asked when Thad hadn't said anything for a moment.

"Yah, danke," Thad replied in Pennsylvania Dutch.

"You seem like you're wrestling with something," Nathan said.

"I am," Thad said. "I know what I need to do, and I want to do it, but I'm terrified."

"That sounds like marriage," Nathan chuckled at his own little joke. "Come on this way. The calf is doing very well. You'll feel better just seeing her."

But it wasn't the calf that was going to soothe Thad's heart today. It was Lydia. He needed to talk things through with her. He needed to hear what she thought of this conviction that was solidifying inside of him. The truths of Christmas were simple, and so was an Old Amish life. Could it be as simple and pure as that?

Because what he felt for Lydia was quite simple, too. He loved her with everything he had.

Chapter Thirteen

"I don't understand why you need to make donuts right now!" Willa said, looking around at the flour-stained counters and the bubbling oil in the cast-iron pan on the woodstove. "Tonight is floor washing, and donuts make quite a mess with all the deep frying. I have a schedule for a reason, Lydia!"

"*Mamm*, this is important," Lydia said. "And I will make up for it this afternoon, I promise. I'll do all the floors myself."

"I'm not asking you to do that," Willa said. "It's almost Christmas. I'll mop behind you. Is this about Thad?"

Lydia felt her cheeks heat, but she hoped her mother would think it was just the heat of the stove that caused the red in her face.

"*Mamm*, I need to talk to him, and I want to bring donuts," she said. "That's all."

"If you must," Willa said. "But I have a fresh cherry pie right there on the counter, and you're welcome to it."

"She can't bring a man her mother's baking," Art said, coming into the room. "I understand that part well enough."

There would be no privacy at all, would there? But her

parents meant well, and for the first time since setting eyes on Thad Miller, Art was finally being supportive.

Lydia was only making a small batch of donuts—a bit of a waste of all that deep frying, she had to admit—but she didn't have much time, either. If she was going to catch Thad at the B&B, she'd better hurry.

An hour later, Lydia took the buggy out to the Draschel B&B, but when she arrived she found that Thad had already packed his things and left.

"I'm sorry," Claire said. "He paid the bill in full and he drove away."

He was gone? Lydia felt the tears rising. Was that it? Was there to be no parting of the Red Sea for her? It was possible, she knew.

"I'll call him, then," Lydia said. "Where is your phone hut?"

"Down the road east," Claire said. "About a half mile."

The donuts had chilled and were cold now as Lydia drove the buggy out to the phone hut. But her heart had started to sink. What was she thinking? Many men lied to women—claimed to love them far more than they did. Was she making a fool of herself? He'd left! Maybe that was the end of it for him, and here she was making donuts like a girl right off her Rumspringa!

She reined in next to the little white hut and she went inside, pulled up the stool and dialed the number from the card.

"Hello, Thad Miller," his deep voice said.

"Thad? This is Lydia, I—"

"Where are you?" he asked. "I'm at your place. Your parents said you just left."

Her heart fluttered in relief. He'd gone to find her... Maybe she wasn't so foolish, after all.

"I'm at the phone hut by the B&B," she said.

"Okay—that's close. Stay there. I'll come to you." She heard his more distanced voice thanking her parents, then the slam of a truck door and the rumble of the engine. "I'm on my way."

Lydia hung up the phone and went back to her buggy. She stood there for a moment, her heart feeling like it was hovering. The cold wind blew, curling around her legs, and she shivered, moving closer to the horse for warmth. About five minutes later she saw headlights and a silver pickup truck heading her way, and she looked down at the donuts. This felt silly suddenly—her and her donuts.

The truck stopped, the engine turned off and Thad hopped out. He strode over to where she stood and he pulled her solidly into his arms.

"Promising not to kiss you until you asked me to was really foolish on my part," he said with a low laugh. "What's in the bag?"

"I made donuts," she said.

"You..." He swallowed. "You said you'd make donuts for your husband."

She nodded. "I know. But I made some for you."

"I don't want to take them under false pretenses," he said. "But here's the thing. I love you, and I want to marry you."

She held her breath. This was the catch, wasn't it? This was where what they wanted failed to matter and it all fell apart.

"I'm Old Order," she said softly, and she looked up

at him, memorizing those soft brown eyes and the faint stubble across his chin.

"I want to join the church," he said. "I want to take Dr. Ted's business offer, be the veterinarian for these parts, and I want to do the job with a horse and buggy. I want to live a plain life with you. I want to marry you, and have children with you, and grow old with you. I want to hitch up your buggy for the rest of my days, if you'll let me."

Tears misted her eyes, and she nodded. "*Yah*. I'll let you!"

"Does that mean you'll marry me?" he asked earnestly.

"*Yah*, I'll marry you."

His gaze dropped down to her lips. "Are you going to ask me to kiss you yet?"

"I'd like that kiss," she said, and she felt her cheeks blaze.

Without another word, Thad pulled her closer into his arms and lowered his warm lips over hers. She felt his kiss right down to the tips of her toes, and she twined her free arm around his neck, her other hand still clutching that bag of donuts. His kiss was lingering and filled with love, and when he finally pulled back, Lydia was breathless. She couldn't believe that all of her prayers had been answered in this one Beachy Amish man.

"I think I can eat those donuts now," Thad said, "in all good conscience."

Lydia would marry him, and she already knew that she'd be reserving her special donuts for him and for the *kinner* that *Gott* would bless them with. She'd saved up a lot of love for the man she'd marry, and she couldn't wait to pour it out on him for the rest of their lives.

"Tomorrow is Christmas Eve," Lydia said.

"I don't know about you, but this is the best Christmas gift I could have asked for," Thad said. "God just keeps on giving..."

"I love you, Thad," she whispered.

"I love you, too." He pecked her lips.

"That leaves just one question," Lydia said with a little smile toying at her lips. "Are you ready to face my parents?"

Epilogue

This Christmas was a very special one for Lydia Speicher. Normally, an engagement stayed a strict secret until about two weeks before the wedding. That was how they did things in the Old Order community. There were preparations still—Thad had to take the baptismal course with an elder before he could be brought into the church, Art and Willa wanted to get to know him better if he was joining the family, and Lydia still needed to properly meet Thad's family, too. There were wedding plans to make on top of all that—but Lydia couldn't keep her secret.

Besides, Adel, Naomi, Claire, Sarai, Delia and Verna were her very closest friends, and Lydia couldn't wait to tell them her news. They'd been on the same journey she had—hoping for love and marriage, and finally finding the man each one couldn't live without. And what a gift that kind of love was! Never to be taken for granted.

Naomi and Mose had come for a visit from Ohio, and Sarai and Arden were back in Redemption for Christmas, too, so it was the perfect time to get the seven of them together at Adel's house on Second Christmas—the day after Christmas Day that was used for more visiting and festivities.

When Lydia arrived at Adel's farmhouse, it was lit from top to bottom and glowed with good cheer. Children were playing on the stairs and thumping overhead. The men had gathered in the sitting room where they chatted and laughed together. There was the smell of cookies from the oven, and the table was piled high with all sorts of tasty treats.

Lydia arrived with Thad—now properly outfitted in Old Amish clothes. It had taken some borrowing, but they'd managed it.

The women exclaimed when she came inside, and they came over to give her a hug. Thad gave Lydia's hand a squeeze and then headed into the sitting room to introduce himself to the men there. Lydia had no doubt that he'd get along just fine. Thad was likable, and he was going to be their local veterinarian, too. Besides, Amish men liked nothing more than giving advice, and Thad would need plenty.

"Wait—" Naomi, who was the last one to give Lydia a side-hug since she had her red-headed baby girl on her hip, looked in the direction Thad had gone. "Is that the Beachy Amish veterinarian I've been hearing about?"

"Hold on…" Adel said, and she turned to Delia's teen-aged stepdaughter with a warm smile. "Violet, can I let you take the baby upstairs and just check on the *kinner* for me? I'm not sure if all that noise is just good fun or an accident waiting to happen."

"Of course I can," Violet said. She loved minding the younger ones, and she loved having a baby to tend even better. She scooped up baby Levi and snuggled him close. "I can tell when there's about to be adult talk."

Violet cast them a rueful smile as she headed up the stairs, and Delia laughed good-naturedly.

The story came out—how Lydia and Thad had met, how their feelings for each other had grown, and how Thad had decided to join the Old Order Amish church and marry Lydia. Adel's eyes widened, and then she jumped from her chair and flung her arms around Lydia.

"*Gott* is the best matchmaker!" Adel said. "Now come sit down and tell us every last detail. We are all vowed to complete secrecy. You know that."

"So how do your parents feel about this?" Delia asked, leaning forward.

"They know he's the right one for me," Lydia replied. "And my *daet* is just so thrilled that he's joining the church. He's determined to teach Thad everything about Old Order living himself."

"And his parents?" Verna asked.

"They're Beachy Amish," Lydia replied. "We went there Christmas Day. We actually took the truck... Thad isn't baptized yet, and it was really important that we tell them together, or feelings would be hurt. His parents are happy for us. They're a little confused about him joining the Old Order church, but they do understand how much we love each other, and his mother is just thrilled that we'll be married soon. We left the truck with them, and his dad actually drove us back to Redemption and dropped us off at the B&B."

"*Yah*, he did!" Claire said with a laugh. "He's a very nice man. I liked him a lot."

"No more driving temptations from now on," Lydia said with a chuckle. "From here on out, it's Old Order ways. That's what Thad said."

As snow started to fall outside, spinning past the window, and as the children played noisily upstairs, and the women passed the babies around the circle, everyone getting a chance to love the littlest ones, Lydia felt the joy and depth of the moment.

This Christmas, her deepest yearnings had been fulfilled in the form of that Beachy Amish veterinarian who'd turned her whole life upside down.

"Do you have any advice for me?" Lydia asked as Naomi's daughter, Hannah Marie, was passed into her lap.

"Advice?" Adel looked around at the other women. "What do we tell a woman soon to be married?"

"Trust his good intentions," Claire said. "It's so easy for us women to get our feelings hurt because he doesn't do things the way we expect. But if you know he loves you, then he really does have the best at heart. Trust that."

There was a murmur of agreement.

"Listen more than you talk," Naomi said. "That's easier said than done, but you've got to let him have his say, too. And nothing is decided until you both are happy."

"And I'd add that you should flirt with your husband—right, Delia?" Verna said with a chuckle. "I finally get to give that advice, but it's so true! He's the only one you can flirt with, so enjoy him."

Delia laughed. "That's the best advice I can give, too!"

"I'd say to not be afraid to have some adventures together, just the two of you," Sarai said. "Going to Ohio was the biggest adventure of my life, but Arden and I are so much closer because we have to rely on each other. It's good for a marriage."

"What about you, Adel?" Lydia asked.

Their matchmaker smiled mistily. "I don't know what to say… I'm just so happy that you are all so happy." She wiped at a tear on her cheek. "All right, this is my advice—always go to *Gott* first. Not to us, not to your mother, not to anyone else! If you and your husband are having difficulties of any kind, take it to *Gott*. He will show you a solution. He always does."

From the sitting room, the sound of the men singing "Away in a Manger" rumbled to life, and Lydia's heart filled to overflowing. She was getting married…it was hard to fully believe still, since it was so new, but she was well and truly marrying the man she loved!

Christmas was about those deeper needs, that fuller love, and the simple things in life that lasted. Money would spend. New things would get old. Christmas gatherings like this one would be forgotten in time…but true love would survive anything that life threw at them.

As Lydia would spend her days loving Thad, every chore she did, every task she undertook would be bathed in prayer. And all those thousands and thousands of prayers would be for her marriage, her family, her friends, her community… But mostly for Thad. Because just like the man who married her would be the recipient of her donuts, he'd be on the receiving end of all those prayers she had stored up, too.

"You are the very best friends a woman could ask for," Lydia said, smiling fondly at these very special women. "May *Gott* bless us all."

* * * * *

Dear Reader,

Writing this last book in the Amish Country Matches miniseries was bittersweet for me. I loved writing Lydia's story, but I was sad to say goodbye to this little community of Redemption, Pennsylvania. If you haven't read all of the books, I hope you'll look them up!

If you enjoyed this story, I hope you'll consider posting a review. I am truly grateful for every review that's posted, because it helps get my books into the hands of new readers, and that in turn keeps me writing these stories for you. I couldn't do this without you!

If you'd like to connect with me, come and find me on social media. I love hearing from my readers. I'd love to stay connected with you through my monthly newsletter. I have monthly giveaways and you'll stay up to date with all of my new releases.

Merry Christmas!

Patricia